CHRISTMAS EVERY DAY

CHRISTMAS EVERY DAY

An Amish Romance

LINDA BYLER

Good Books

New York, New York

CHRISTMAS EVERY DAY

Good Books books may be purchased in bulk at special discounts for sales promotion, corporate gifts, fund-raising, or educational purposes. Special editions can also be created to specifications. For details, contact the Special Sales Department, Good Books, 307 West 36th Street, 11th Floor, New York, NY 10018 or info@skyhorsepublishing.com.

Good Books is an imprint of Skyhorse Publishing, Inc.®, a Delaware corporation.

Visit our website at www.goodbooks.com.

10 9 8 7 6 5 4 3 2 1

Library of Congress Cataloging-in-Publication Data

Names: Byler, Linda, author.
Title: Christmas every day : an Amish romance / Linda Byler.
Description: New York, New York : Good Books, [2023] | Summary: "A heartwarming tale set in Amish country at Christmastime"-- Provided by publisher.
Identifiers: LCCN 2023020543 (print) | LCCN 2023020544 (ebook) | ISBN 9781680998955 (print) | ISBN 9781680999013 (ebook)
Subjects: LCSH: Amish--Fiction. | LCGFT: Romance fiction. | Christian fiction. | Christmas fiction. | Novels.
Classification: LCC PS3602.Y53 C46 2023 (print) | LCC PS3602.Y53 (ebook) | DDC 813/.6--dc23/eng/20230501
LC record available at https://lccn.loc.gov/2023020543
LC ebook record available at https://lccn.loc.gov/2023020544

Print ISBN: 978-1-68099-895-5
eBook ISBN: 978-1-68099-901-3

Cover design by Create Design Publish LLC

Printed in the United States of America

They keep Christmas all the year.

—William Walker (1672)

CHRISTMAS EVERY DAY

Chapter One

IN THE HILLS OF KENTUCKY, BETWEEN TWO fairly high ridges covered in all manner of trees and flowering shrubs, fallen logs and mushrooms, moss and decayed leaves leftover from last year, a river wound its way along the base, a ribbon of greenish brown water loaded with silt, pebbles, rocks, and fish. Not too far away, the rolling terrain leveled off to an expanse of farm land, crops growing in neat if uneven patches, like a crazy quilt, where one single patch is not perfect but is made to fit in with all the rest.

Red barns and concrete silos with white or beige or gray farmhouses punctuated the landscape, with undulating roads winding along every which way, some of them macadam with yellow lines down the middle, but many of them covered in gravel, cross-hatched with potholes deep enough to jar your teeth if you were riding on a steel-rimmed buggy wheel attached to the body of the buggy itself.

The sky above was blue as far as you could see, with loose clouds blowing along on the summer breeze, scattering wherever they wanted, creating many shapes and forms. Heat hung just below them, the sun's rays creating a pocket of discomfort for man and beast as the mercury on the rusted white thermometer on Mam's wheel line post rose to ninety-eight degrees.

Annie and Fannie, the twins, were instructed by Mam herself to bring the clean, dry laundry in, fold it, and put it away. They considered themselves much too young to accomplish a task of this size, but when Mam's face turned red, her nostrils flared slightly, and she spoke louder than normal, you did what you were told, no question.

Fannie was the older, by a few minutes, and she weighed five pounds more. Her hair was thicker and her face rounder, so she considered herself superior, which seemed to serve as a bellows for a slow-burning fire where her twin was concerned. Annie was thin as a reed, her face without the full rounded cheeks of her sister, so folks could tell them apart easily, although they were identical twins. Dark-haired, dark-eyed, brown as an acorn, and cute as a button, they wore identical dresses every day, their bare feet callused from their wandering around the many fields, woods, creeks, and ponds in which they found adventure.

The only downside of their happy-go-lucky existence was the great number of older siblings that inhabited the enormous farmhouse. Ten of them, and no twins except themselves, which in their opinion should have given them more status, a bit of special treatment, of which they were sadly lacking.

"Fannie do this, Annie do that. Get me a drink, fetch me some ice. Oh, we're out of applesauce. Fannie, get a jar of applesauce. Annie, we need ketchup. Run quick."

At the age of ten, it seemed their primary value to the family was in running here, running there. Their only chance at freedom was some of these bossy siblings finding someone, anyone, to marry so they'd leave the home. But the way it appeared, there was no chance of anyone even thinking about moving out. No boyfriends or girlfriends, nothing. Older brothers were the biggest trouble of all, especially when it came to laundry. All these denim trousers, an endless line of colorful button-down shirts, heavy socks that took forever to dry.

Mam was a very good kind of mother, but she favored those big dark-haired galumphs, walking through the house in their stocking feet, leaving wet, muddy, or manure-encrusted shoes lying haphazardly on the kettlehouse floor, walking like elephants and taking up as much room. Mike and Amos could be married by now, but showed no interest, which meant Annie and Fannie were pretty much stuck being gofers. Dat laughed and laughed about that, and neither Fannie nor Annie thought it was slightly humorous. They just rolled their eyes at each other and felt very misunderstood, very servantly.

When it was time to get the long line of laundry in, they took turns standing on tiptoe to draw the line to the back porch where they took off the clothespins and dropped the clothes in the huge Rubbermaid clothes basket. Mam was mowing grass, the mower purring along as she walked behind it, leaving a swath of neatly cut lawn.

Sarah was at work, cleaning an English (non-Amish) lady's house, while Becky and Mary snapped green beans on the front porch. There was always work to be done, always someone coming or going, especially in summer when school was over.

Fannie threw a handful of clothes in the basket, then told Annie it was her turn, her legs were tired from standing on her tiptoes. Annie looked at the height of the line, then got a sturdy patio chair, hoisted it into position, and stepped up on it. She reached way out to grasp the line and upset the chair, crashing down on the cement floor, scattering clothespins everywhere. Landing on her side, she lay motionless, howling.

"Annie! Are you alright? My goodness." Fannie tried to help her up, but Annie swatted her away, rolled over, and continued howling. Fannie watched as Annie sat up, gripped her shoulder and made horrible grimaces, her face contorted in pain.

"Did you break your arm?"

When there was no answer, only an increase in the awful noise coming out of her throat, Fannie ran across the yard and waved down her mother, who shut off the mower, took one look at Annie, and hurried to the porch, perspiration rolling off her very red face.

"Annie, hush. It's okay. Come. Let me see if it's broken."

She manipulated the arm tenderly, then wiped her face with the corner of her apron, said it was time for them all to take a break. The lawn mower sat in the middle of the lawn, the clothes stayed in the basket, and the bushel of string beans on the front porch sat unfinished as Mam poured tall plastic glasses of meadow tea for everyone. Ruth and Naomi came in from the barn, their arms and legs scratched from helping with the hay.

"What happened to you, Annie?"

Annie didn't answer, but just sniffed and went inside for a Kleenex. She blew her nose with a mighty honk, wiped her eyes, and went back out for her own glass of meadow tea. She was ready to slide into her place by the picnic table when Mam said, "Pretzels would be good."

Annie pretended not to have heard. So did Fannie.

After a while, Mam sighed, heaved out of the chair, and went inside.

"Why didn't one of you go? Mam is tired. Didn't you see her mowing grass?" Becky asked.

Fannie glared and Annie sniffed, rubbing her shoulder. Neither of them said anything. They drank their tea, then got down the rest of the clothes—without the use of the chair—and went inside to fold them, leaving Mam and the big girls to talk about important subjects, things they knew didn't include them at all.

Fannie pulled a pair of denims off the pile, held them up before tucking the waistband beneath her chin as she brought the side pockets to their position along the inside back. She folded them, slapped them on the pile, and reached for another. Every pair was marked with the owner's initial on the inside of the waistband, taking out the guesswork of which pair belonged to whom.

Suddenly Fannie said, "I'm not going to have twelve children when I get married. It's too much laundry."

"I'm never marrying, so that takes care of that," Annie answered.

"Go get the towels and tablecloths."

"You go. It's hot, and I hurt my shoulder."

Fannie went. Annie matched socks, folded them, and placed them on the piles of trousers and shirts. Even the underwear was initialed, but not the socks. They had to wear whatever was put in their drawer.

By suppertime, the yard was mowed, the beans bubbled in the agate canner, laundry was folded and put away. Fried chicken was in the oven, tomatoes sliced, zucchini squash fried, and a huge platter of golden ears of corn waited to be taken outside to the picnic table. Mam moved around the kitchen like an efficient work engine, barking orders, handing out ice cube trays and pitchers of meadow tea. Dat and the boys were filthy with sweat and hay dust, their faces black with it, their hands dark and callused. Their eyes danced as they jostled for position at the sink in the kettlehouse, rolling the green lava soap around in their palms before scrubbing, then drying their hands on the brown towel beside it.

"Come on, Mike. You're not getting ready to do surgery. Hurry it up."

Towels were snapped, backsides turned quickly, shoulders punched. Everyone slid into place along the two picnic tables on the back porch of the mammoth white farmhouse, the old oak tree casting deep shadows, the breeze toying with thick leaves, bringing a bit of cooling air to the heat-soaked bodies. Hummingbirds flitted from the red feeder to the hosta blossoms and back again, sparrows chirping from nests in the wooden eaves of the tool shed beyond the garden. Cows lowed softly by the white board fence, the red metal on the barn creating a picturesque scene straight out of a rural American painting.

Doves cooed from the electric wire, and barn swallows dove into the open door of the barn, the source of contention among the boys and their father. Dat loved barn swallows, said they helped with the fly population, but the boys did not like the nests in the ceiling, the inevitable pile of bird excrement on the floor of the forebay. They muttered to themselves as they took scraper and broom to the mess.

But the swallow problem was the last thing on their minds as they all waited till Dat asked if they were ready for the silent prayer, then bowed their heads in unison, after which they helped themselves to Mam's delicious supper.

Four dozen ears of corn, twenty pieces of chicken, four cast iron pans of fried zucchini and six whole tomatoes, gallons of meadow tea. Bread and mayonnaise, loaded down with zucchini rounds and tomato.

"Butter!"

"Who has the salt?"

Dat raised his eyebrows. "What happened to *please* and *thank you*?"

"Oh, sorry. May I please have the salt after you're done emptying the whole shaker on one ear of corn?"

"Yes, kind sir. You may. There are still a few granules for your consumption, thank you."

Laughter rippled along the benches. Fannie looked sideways at Annie and grinned. Suppertime was always something to look forward to, a time to listen to the big boys and Dat, hear about the day's farming, in haying season especially. Sometimes the twins were allowed to drive the team of plodding Belgians, but only Dan and Tom, the two oldest and most trustworthy.

Dat sat back, full of good food. His eyes were crinkly, set deep beneath bushy eyebrows, his forehead pale in comparison to the rest of his deeply tanned face. His dark hair and beard were fringed in gray and white.

"We got some high-quality hay in the barn today," he said, finding his wife's eyes on his face.

She smiled, and he smiled back. "A good feeling for you. Certainly a blessing from the Lord."

"Yep, sure is. My dat used to say we need to thank God for every load that goes into the barn. Hear that, boys?"

Nods of assent, distant "yeahs."

It was scary, though, these wagons loaded heavily with bales of hay, clattering on steel wheels lurching up the incline into the bank barn, the Belgians' haunches lowered as they leaned into their collars, immense hooves digging in as they drew the great load up and over the cement threshold of the great old barn. They'd make their way into the dark interior, the air thick with the pungent scent of freshly baled hay, shafts of light coming through high windows in the gable ends, the heavy floorboards able to hold the massive horses, the mighty load of hay balanced on steel wheels. Not all of them were drawn into the barn, only the first loads. When there was no more room, an elevator was placed on the incline, the gasoline engine chugging faithfully as the bales of hay went up, up, up to tumble into the bay to be packed tightly with the rest. And that wasn't the only thing that was scary. If Dat was sloppy or miscalculated the moisture in the mown and raked hay, it could heat up to a high degree, actually starting a hay fire in the barn during the night. Sometimes Annie couldn't go to sleep thinking about it.

Things like that didn't bother Fannie, who could snore through all kinds of summer thunderstorms or talk of war or new presidents or climate change, while Annie read the newspaper and felt a dull tingling in her stomach about the war in Ukraine. She also thought about every parking lot and freeway covered in blacktop and concrete and all the heat that would throw off, not to mention men hacking away at the rainforest and all the cars and airplanes and trucks and buses putting out all that stuff in the air, whatever it was. She told Fannie about this not too long ago, and Fannie told her not to be ridiculous, which really made Annie hopping mad, just the way she said it. She smacked her lightly on her forearm and told her to quit it, too, which really didn't do any good, but still.

She sat up, held very still, and stopped chewing. Dat was talking about signs of the end of the world. Her stomach lurched. Why did he have to say such things at the supper table? She excused herself and went to the bathroom and stayed there for a very long time before venturing out to the screen door to listen.

"We have nothing to be afraid of. Not one single thing. We are *fa-sarked* (taken care of) by our faith in the end times."

Words like honey. Soothing and sweet. Annie sat back down at her space along the picnic table and didn't answer Fannie when she asked where she was.

After everything was cleared away, dishes washed, and the porch swept, it was time to feed calves. There were eight of them, all in their own white hutch with a small woven wire enclosure. It was not nearly enough space, Annie told Fannie, who told her she thought of the most unnecessary things. The calves were perfectly alright until they were done being bottle-fed, but Annie thought they should be able to run and kick up their heels the way they did years ago. But they were happy to see Annie and Fannie approach with the big plastic bottles with the brick-colored nipples. Their eyes were large and gentle, and sometimes they were sad, she didn't care what Fannie said. Calves had feelings, too.

After the white calf starter powder was mixed with warm water, they filled the bottles and hooked them to a special hook made for that purpose, except for a few who had to be hand-fed, the bossy ones who bucked the bottle too hard. All the barn cats hung around, waiting for their dish of milk, so Fannie sat in the grass and petted their silky backs as they arched against her, purring. Annie was okay with cats, but she never petted them the way Fannie did. Cats had parasites and sore eyes, and their bathroom habits were deplorable.

When the animals were fed, the twins were allowed to play in the creek, but they weren't allowed to swim in the pond unless Becky or Mary or Sarah accompanied them. They could swim like fish, all of them, so it made no sense that they couldn't swim without the older girls, Annie and Fannie thought, but it was Dat's rule. Mam's too.

So tonight they had to be content to splash in the creek, way back behind the corncrib, down the dirt lane and across the hay field that was nothing but scratchy stubbles. They had to wear shoes so they wouldn't hurt their feet. The big girls were allowed to wear flip-flops, but Annie and Fannie weren't. It was not even remotely fair what these *rumschpringa* (teenage Amish) got away with, but at only ten years old, no one asked the twins what they thought.

They lifted their skirts and waded up to their knees, then tucked them between their legs to bend over and watch minnows darting in and out of the shadows. They were impossible to catch without a net, so they watched a while, till they got bored, then dared each other to lift big rocks and look for salamanders and snakes. They slipped on moss-covered rocks, fell into the shallow water, and sat down with the ripples going past their waists. It was delightfully refreshing after the heat of the day.

"Guess what I heard Mike say to Mam?" Fannie said in that tone meaning she was much better and smarter than Annie herself.

Annie feigned disinterest, spread her hands, and watched the water flow between her fingers.

"Did you hear me?"

"Yeah. 'Course."

"Well, he told Mam if he only had the nerve to ask Miriam, every day would be like Christmas if she say yes. Imagine! Every day would be like Christmas. Surely it wouldn't be that good, just sitting beside your girlfriend and talking to her on the weekend. I'd much rather have real Christmas."

"Me too." Annie considered this, then asked, "Which Miriam?"

"I don't know. Not Miriam Stoltzfus in our church. I hope not. She's way too pretty for him."

"Who cares? He probably won't do it."

"You want to know what Mam told him?"

Annie shrugged.

"Don't you?"

"Not really."

"Why ever not?"

"I'm never getting married, so it's no concern of mine."

"Well, I am fully planning on it, so it's interesting. She told him to pray about it. Pray. How would you do that? Like, *please let me have Miriam*, or how?"

"I have no idea."

"But imagine having Christmas every day."

"It's too hot to think about Christmas, Fannie. And besides, you shouldn't be eavesdropping on Mam."

They walked home together, their shoes squishing water, their skirts sticking to their legs, cooled down and ready for a quick shower and cold watermelon. Annie said Mam was taking them school shopping next week, which was terribly exciting. Maybe even more exciting than Christmas. Fannie lifted her face to the streaks of navy blue clouds resting in the yellow glow of the orange sun sinking behind dark mountains and groaned.

"I don't want to think about it yet. Arithmetic is too hard. I'd much rather be in the kitchen with Mam. She showed me how to fill the cupcake liners just right so they don't run over. It takes lots of practice, but I'm getting better."

"Good. I hate to bake."

"I know. Nothing wrong with that."

Fannie took her hand and squeezed. "We're identical twins, but not so identical inside, are we?"

They looked at each other, smiled, and nodded.

An observer from behind would have been able to capture an unforgettable image, one of two sisters holding hands with sodden rose-colored dresses, their dark hair pulled into small buns on the backs of their heads, their faces toward each other as they walked.

Two peas in a pod.

But at ten years old, they were establishing differences already, developing their own personalities, their separate likes and dislikes.

Their parents were so involved in the older children's lives and in the church and community, and with the endless cycle of hard work on the farm, that Annie and Fannie became a small island to themselves, secure in who they were and what they were about. Often, they were the least of both parents' concern.

Twelve children. It was a great honor, a God-given gift of abundance, and Ben and his wife Malinda thanked Him every day for this responsibility entrusted to them. They sought His guidance to raise them according to His will. But Mike was getting up in age, nearing thirty, and behind him were a string of unmarried children growing into adulthood. But what was there to say or do?

In good time, it would happen.

Chapter Two

FANNIE DASHED DOWN THE WIDE UPSTAIRS hallway, tore into their bedroom, and hissed, "Annie, put that book down this minute. Come on, you have to go with me."

Annie lay the book aside, bent down the top of the page, and closed it. "What?" Her tone let Fannie know she was annoyed.

"I was putting laundry away in Mike's room. Come quick."

Annie swung her legs over the side of the bed and got to her feet.

"Hurry up," Fannie hissed.

Mike shared a room with Amos, two double beds with a night stand between them. On top of it, propped against the battery lamp, was a blue envelope, not yet sealed. Fannie extracted lined writing paper folded neatly, also in blue.

"Look. Read it. Quick."

Annie's eyes traveled back and forth across the page. Her mouth dropped open. "He asked her on paper?"

"Yeah. A letter. What is he thinking? I mean, it's not 1950."

"Maybe he simply doesn't have the nerve to approach her face to face. I kind of pity him. He's old. Too old to ask someone like her. I just wish he had better handwriting. It's so sad."

They sat on the bed, side by side. Fannie sighed, then got to her feet, took the basket of clean laundry to the dressers and proceeded to put things in drawers.

Annie watched, chewing her lower lip. "Why couldn't he call her at least?"

"I don't know."

Both looked up at once, knowing it was time to take this matter seriously.

"We'll talk to him," Fannie said.

Annie nodded.

* * *

A few days later, they cornered the unsuspecting Mike in the barn where he was loading baler twine into a wheelbarrow to take to the burn pile. Dat kept a meticulous barn and taught his boys well.

"Mike?"

He turned, grinned. "What's up with my best twins?"

Very seriously, they placed their hands behind their backs and said, "We think you've made a bit of a mistake."

"What?" he laughed. He pulled out a bale of hay and sat on it.

"Okay, don't be insulted now," Fannie began.

"I won't." But he was still smiling.

"You should not write to Miriam Stoltzfus. You need to ask her the normal way. Like, ask her outright," Fannie said, stammering only a little.

"And how, may I ask, do you know anything about this?"

Fannie told him. Annie nodded.

He grimaced, looked embarrassed for only a second, then asked how they had the nerve to read it.

They should not be allowed to snoop into other siblings' business.

"You're too old for her."

He eyed them with a comical expression, then burst out laughing. He caught his breath, slapped his knee, and started a fresh laugh.

"Little snoops is what you are. It's not the Miriam in our church district. There's another one more suited to my style. Over by Donaldsburg. She's here teaching school."

They breathed in through their noses, exhaled through their mouths, then told him it was a great relief. They simply didn't want to see him be disappointed, and also, it probably wasn't a great idea comparing his life with her to Christmas, seeing how Christmas wasn't all that great as you became older.

He laughed even harder, thanked them for looking out for him. They heard him whistle as he left through the barn door with the wheelbarrow full of twine.

* * *

Mam took the four girls school shopping, so the blue letter and its contents was laid to rest, their time taken up with dress fittings, new black belt aprons, choosing sneakers and new sweaters, plus notebooks, colored pencils, crayons, and all the things they would need to begin the school year. Annie was thrilled, Fannie not so much, with Ruth and Naomi—the big girls in sixth and eighth grade—acting as if they were much too cool for their excitement, shrugging their shoulders about sneakers, snorting about Mam's choice of sweaters until she spoke quite firmly to them.

She took them out for dinner at Hardee's, a place smelling of French fries and smoked meat. Annie's eyes welled with unexpected tears when she drank Coke through a straw, unaccustomed to soda of any kind. She was ashamed and swiped furiously at her eyes, turning her face away from Naomi, but was comforted when Mam smiled and patted her shoulder. The French fries were piping hot, salty and delicious, especially with small paper cups of ketchup to dip them in.

When they got home, Mike was bouncing around as if there were springs in his feet. He could barely wait till Mam was in the house before telling her about his Sunday night.

Annie and Fannie hid behind the gray recliner and heard every single word.

His little sisters had given him some advice, and he took it. He had simply walked up to her when she was helping her brother hitch up and asked if he could come see her Saturday evening. She'd said yes. Yes, he could. Oh, he was happy. He was in the clouds. Cloud nine. On top of the world. Mam congratulated him, told him she was happy, too.

"Where are Annie and Fannie?" he asked.

"I have no idea. We just got back."

They hunkered behind the recliner and held palms to their mouths to keep from laughing. They managed to stay quiet, except for a few squeaks which could easily have been mistaken for a mouse.

They stood side by side on Saturday afternoon when he washed his buggy, ran willingly to bring the glass cleaner and paper towels when he needed them, generally in awe of every move he made. Ruth and

Naomi stayed away, except they made quite a few trips to the milkhouse, which Annie and Fannie discussed in secret. They guaranteed there was not one single thing they needed in that milkhouse, they were just excited about Mike's first date.

When he dressed up in his Sunday best, they all agreed he looked very nice, and Dat might or might not have wiped a few stray tears. Thirty years old and finally dating.

* * *

That Sunday morning, Mam breathed heavily as she yanked the hairbrush through the girls' hair, wet it with the plastic spritz bottle, and rolled the hair alongside their heads as tightly as humanly possible without tearing it out by the roots. When she breathed like that, it meant she was tired, so you had to stay quiet when she poked the hairpins in the bun on back of your head. Otherwise, she'd say "Hush."

White capes and aprons pinned over blue Sunday dresses, white covering on their heads, and they were hustled into the back seat of the buggy, squashed between Ruth and Naomi, who complained the whole way to church about their white capes and aprons being smashed.

Mam said, "Hush now."

Dat sang slow hymns beneath his breath, happy as they'd ever seen him, but Mam dozed off the minute the first sermon began, her head falling lower and lower until Fannie elbowed Annie and whispered for her to look at Mam. She was afraid she'd fall out of her chair.

When Mike told Mam on Monday that his date had been absolutely great, just wonderful, and, yes, he would be seeing her again, Mam breathed out a long silent *whoosh*, slumped in her chair, and began to smile. She sang while she worked the rest of the day. Annie felt sorry for her mother, raising so many children, then going through so much stress before they'd move out.

The dating bug caught on, and Amos asked Sadie Kauffman from way over in Lyonsville, in the north district. She didn't answer him for over a month, which should not have happened in any way, shape, or form, in Dat's words. Mam couldn't take the stress, fearing for Amos, who had always been very softhearted, even in school. If this Sadie said no, he'd be devastated, as cautious as he was.

Fannie and Annie took refuge in the safety of their wooden school desks, away from the whirling dervish that was their mother. Nerves on edge, she yelled when she should have spoken softly, started housecleaning long before she was finished canning, creating a mountain of work she simply couldn't see her way through. They fed calves; peeled pears and neck pumpkins shaped like gigantic gourds, carried jars of pears, applesauce, and pumpkin to the basement; helped clean out the last of the tomatoes and sweet potatoes; and wished for their mother back. Dat did take them aside and said Mam was a little high strung, perhaps, but she loved her children and wanted them to be happy. He gave them each a ten-dollar bill, new and crisp, said he appreciated the good care of the calves. He'd gotten a good price for them at the sale barn. They lifted their shoulders, held their heads a little higher, and gave him a hearty "thank you," then skipped off.

The leaves turned to gold, orange, red, and yellow, but autumn in Kentucky was mellow and warm. Annie wore a sweater to walk to school in the morning, but Fannie chose not to, saying the sun would burn through the chilly fog soon enough.

And when Sadie Kauffman finally gave Amos her answer, Mam was like a deflated balloon, relaxing in her chair in the evening, becoming teary-eyed at every little thing. She played games of Sorry or Uno with them, told them Bible stories from the blue books, and thanked God every evening for Sadie Kauffman's quiet "yes."

"Oh my," she told her buddies at the quilting. Two boys dating was almost too much happiness. She said it was like Christmas every day, which must have come awfully close to boasting, the way Benuel Zook's wife, Verna, repressed a snort and glared instead, thinking, *Really? You have a whole lineup of older girls who aren't dating yet.* All this was lost on the exuberant Mam, who knew both Miriam's and Sadie's families from various church and community events over the years and found them very much to her liking. She thought, *My oh! Next thing I know these boys will be married and we'll have grandbabies.*

* * *

Annie and Fannie walked to school beneath a canopy of brilliant leaves, scuffling through the fallen ones that created a colorful carpet, the gravel beneath completely covered. Naomi and Ruth walked behind them in their own little world of upper grade goings-on, so the twins could converse freely without correction from their older sisters. Everyone had settled down at home, so the house was back to its gentle, well-ordered rhythm, except for one blossoming catastrophe waiting to happen. Sarah, next in line to Amos, had obviously caught the dating virus, which Annie and Fannie reasoned was a very severe case. She was testy. Just yesterday, she'd chased them out of the bathroom before they were completely finished brushing their teeth, and they had hurried with their showers. Then she'd told them they never cleaned up after themselves, which was not true. They did.

Annie snuck into her room and checked to see if her diary was locked, which it wasn't, springing open at the touch of the small gold clasp.

Aha.

It was exactly what she thought. Oh, my word. Her eyes could not take in the words fast enough. Emanuel. Emanuel this and Emanuel that. He spoke to me. I think he was watching me. What does God have in store for me? Will I be single all the days of my life? Copied poetry, sad, stupid words that made no sense. Whatever. Way far from Christmas every day. Poor thing.

She told Fannie, who pressed a hand to her mouth and opened her eyes so wide Annie was afraid she'd pop a blood vessel.

"Emanuel Beiler!" she shrieked. He was shorter than her, and probably younger. Unless it was a different Emanuel?

In church a week later, they whispered and jammed elbows into each other's sides so much their mother caught their eye and gave them a look that sizzled with disapproval. It was definitely the Emanuel Beiler they knew, who was rather dashing in a chubby sort of way. Not really chubby, just round and jolly, very friendly, sort of a youthful Santa Claus.

But no Christmas joy here. Not yet.

They solemnly agreed to never, ever let the cat out of the bag, and if the name Emanuel ever passed their lips in her presence, they were history. The cold winds of November made them wrap their sweaters tightly around themselves and they set their lunches in the wet leaves to tie their black bonnets a bit tighter. When Ruth and Naomi caught up, they tried to pry the conversation they'd had right out of them, but they were used to their wiles and ran off like jackrabbits.

Teacher Rachel suspected the mischief in them, found them both a bit unruly. When a rubber band was shot to her desk, coming to rest on top of her hardcover answer books, she looked to Annie and Fannie immediately, finding them both bent over sideways, madly scrabbling around in their desks, then lifting scarlet faces of profuse confusion.

Guilty as charged, she thought, and aimed the inevitable question straight at them.

"Annie, was it you?"

"What?"

"This." Holding up the rubber band like a dead mouse. "Did you shoot this to my desk?"

"No. I don't know how to shoot them."

A long piercing look found the dark eyes holding hers quite steadily. Fannie was scrabbling in her desk again.

"Fannie?"

She jumped six inches off her seat.

"Yes?"

"Was it you?"

"It was an accident. I didn't mean to send it to your desk."

"You may both stay sitting when the bell goes for recess."

The gavel had fallen, punishment pronounced. With Ruth and Naomi sitting like aristocrats in the back seat, oozing righteousness, they had not a smidgen of hope. Straight home they'd stalk, burst through the door with exceeding great joy, and tell Mam they had been kept in at recess, which would bring a whole new set of corrections. It wasn't right the way they *lived* to keep Annie and Fannie in line, but as far as they could tell, there wasn't much they could do about it now, as Annie was one hundred percent sure she'd seen Fannie shoot that rubber band with amazing aim. She was the best rubber band shooter in school history.

But with solemn admonition meted out, thick and slow as dark molasses, and as suffocating, they sat like two sticks and absorbed the words falling from the thin mouth of the teacher. They got out their tablets and wrote "I will not shoot rubber bands, and I am sorry" one hundred times. Annie thought it wasn't fair for her to do this, but pitied Fannie to stay in by herself, so she bent her head, bit her tongue, wrote as fast as she possibly could, handed in her paper, and sat down again, hoping her face showed proper respect. She wasn't sorry. She had done nothing, but she knew when to pretend.

And she understood why Fannie did it. Sometimes you had to do something to relieve boredom, or just to feel that silent jiggle in your stomach. A happy shaking of yourself, a little brightness in the middle of an ordinary day.

But when they got home that afternoon, they took one look at the set of Mam's mouth and knew Ruth and Naomi had already tattled.

"Girls!"

Whoa, Annie thought. Her heart jumped in her throat. She looked at Fannie, and Fannie looked at her.

"What do I hear about you?"

Two sets of shoulders slumped, lifted, slumped.

"Is it true you had to stay in for recess?"

"Ya." Solemn nods, sheep's eyes, hoping for mercy.

"Fannie, aren't you ashamed of yourself? Such conduct."

"I didn't mean to hit the teacher's desk, just sort of zing it through the air."

"Why would you do something like that?"

"I guess to watch it go."

Annie saw Mam's mouth twitch and knew the punishment would not be too severe, but as always, Dat had to be told. A misdemeanor in school was serious business, and parents hardly ever took the children's part. They were raised to respect authority, certainly, and a rubber band on a teacher's desk was not good. Neither was staying in for recess.

At the supper table, they weren't too worried, seeing how Dat was in a good mood, laughing and joking about the amount of manure in the horse barn, the boys shaking their heads and grinning. It was a promising sign, so they ate their chicken stew and applesauce with a hearty appetite, not the way food stuck in a dry mouth when you knew you had it coming.

In the barn, when they were measuring calf starter, Dat called them over, looked down at them from a terrible height. Why did parents grow so much taller when they were displeased?

"I hear you misbehaved in school."

"Fannie did. I watched," Annie said quickly.

"Rubber band, huh?"

"Yes. I didn't do it on purpose." Her lips trembled.

"You did; it just didn't land where you wanted it to. Well, it was disobedience, either way, and I'm not happy about it. So I want you two to clean out Mam's tomatoes this evening before it gets dark. Use the garden cart, dump them on the compost pile.

And, Fannie, don't let it happen again. You too, Annie." But his eyes were very kind, although the corners of his mouth never lifted, not even the beginning of a smile.

They were quiet as they fed calves, quiet when they went for the garden cart, but started talking the second they saw the long row of twisted tomato stalks tied to wooden stakes, dripping with rotten tomatoes.

Annie threw herself down in the wet soil and sat there with her face full of despair. She glared at Fannie and told her she wasn't the one who'd thrown that rubber band, so why did she have to help?

"I didn't throw it either, dummy. I shot it. There's a trick to it." She lifted her thumb, pointed an index finger, closed one eye, and sighted along it like a pistol.

"I'm telling on you. We are not allowed to call someone a dummy."

"Well."

"Well what?"

They sat in the garden and had a senseless, fierce argument about nothing, so great was the dread of untying those disgusting stalks. Eventually, they had to face their punishment and get going. The stalks were heavy and hard to handle, but the worst thing, by far, was the slimy rotten tomatoes squishing beneath the soles of their sneakers, falling off the dead vines as they heaved them into the garden cart.

It was hard work and not funny at all. It was getting dark by the time they finished, blue jays yelling and screaming from the pine tree by the pasture gate.

Annie lifted a fist, watched as they flew across the evening sky. She blamed Fannie for this, felt it unfair that she had to help her.

But still.

She had laughed inside, felt that jiggle in her stomach, and was proud of her twin sister, the sharp-shooter.

Chapter Three

CHURCH SERVICES WERE HELD EVERY OTHER week, an old tradition based on the Sunday being free to visit neighboring districts or to have German catechism, the time when Dat took the teaching of the Deutsch Shrift very seriously, gathering his large clan in a somber circle in the living room. But on Sunday mornings before church, the house was thrown into a silent rushing melee of controlled panic.

Coordinating twelve siblings, chores, and breakfast in the span of a few early morning hours was no easy feat. Annie and Fannie had learned early on it was best to stay quiet and out of everyone's path. They knew to hold perfectly still while Mam yanked the brush through their long dark hair, wet it down as severely as a swimming dog, and rolled it so tightly their eyelids lifted in eternal questioning. After that, *Kopp nunna*, which meant they folded their arms on a tabletop, forehead positioned on top, while Mam wound their long thick hair in a bob on the back of their heads, after which she jammed hairpins into them with vicious speed. This, too, was endured patiently, despite the scraping of steel pins along the back of their scalps.

She wasn't finished yet. Out came the white cape and apron, whipped across their shoulders, adjusted, pleats folded and pinned, the belt apron slid around their waists and pins jammed into their back, sometimes pricking them, which was met with an unappreciated yelp, a "Sorry" from Mam, but she was never truly sorry.

"Shoes," she ordered, so they put on black shoes and stockings, as ugly as all get-out, but there was nothing to do about that, as Mam was a real stickler for *ordnung* (Amish rules). Last was the white head covering, drawn over the back of their heads, more pins along the sides to hold them in place, the strings tied beneath their chins, and they were ready except for their black shawls and bonnets.

Ruth and Naomi thought they should do their own hair, since they were getting older, but Mam would not allow it, so there was always grumbling, or at least the start of a resistance, quickly put to rest by a few quick words from Mam.

Annie and Fannie tried to hide their glee, but inwardly they were very pleased the way Mam cut them off. They were getting too big for their britches, those two, and Mam was smart enough to detect it.

This morning, they didn't want to wear their shawls and bonnets, saying it wasn't cold enough, and that the bonnet smashed their covering. Mam told them they had no idea what a smashed covering was, then told them about the Swiss organdy fabric everyone used to wear before the new, better fabric came into use.

"Why can't we go without? By the time we're all piled into the back, we'll be warm enough," they whined.

But the stack of black shawls and bonnets were brought from the closet shelf and put on and they were sent out the door like a herd of yearling heifers, arranged on the back seat, Ruth and Naomi snorting and squealing about their aprons being creased, Annie and Fannie shrinking as much as possible in the narrow space on the back seat.

Dat and Mam never said anything about the older girls bossing them around, which didn't seem fair, but that was the way life was when you were the smallest girls in the family. They had accepted a long time ago when they leaned on the fence watching the litter of piggies jockeying for position, the smallest always unable to get their fair share of milk, that humans weren't that different from animals at all.

They were the runts of the litter too.

But by the time they reached the place where church services were held, everything had calmed down, Dat's low voice humming one of the *lieda*, the songs being sung that day. He was always one of the men who willingly announced a page, then led the singing in his clear baritone. He never fumbled the way some of the younger ones did, which made the twins feel proud.

They followed their mother to the spacious, well-lit shop, found the designated area for outerwear, divested themselves of the cumbersome shawls and bonnets before joining their friends, standing against a table, smiling, saying their good mornings shyly. It was one thing to say hello in school, but it was more formal in church, with all the big girls intimidating them that way. They stood quietly, sizing up the *rumschpringa* (older teenage) girls, especially the fancy ones who wore short sleeves and had their hair rolled on top of their heads. They were really something, these girls. Mam shook her head but didn't say much at all, her mouth in a straight line, her eyes bunched up the way they did when she disapproved, reminding the girls they were subject to formidable rules and regulations coming straight from their mother's conservative view.

Today, Cheryl Stoltzfus wore a brilliant peach color, a color Annie and Fannie said later was even prettier than the zinnias in Mam's garden. There was no hope of ever wearing that color themselves, but it was nice to admire it on someone else. They looked down at their own navy blue dresses with the sleeves to their wrists, hemmed straight and in the *ordnung* for little girls.

Sarah and Becky King were their best friends, so when they arrived, they stood in a tight group, giggling, whispering things they didn't want the other girls to hear. One was the ongoing mystery of another rubber band shooting in school, which no one could blame on the twins anymore.

Fannie put a hand to her mouth and said she knew who it was, but there was no way she would tell. Annie's eyes opened wide, she thrust an elbow into her sister's side, and said if she supported the shooter, it was the same as doing it herself.

"Nuh-uh," Fannie said, justifying herself.

"Yes, it is. You know it, too."

Sarah laughed quietly, but nodded her head in agreement.

They turned as one to shake hands with Lizzie Glick, a girl in eighth grade who often gave them their arithmetic flash cards.

Lizzie was pretty big, fat, actually, and funny, so everybody loved her. When they were allowed to have flashcards on the porch, they didn't behave at all, with no one to see. They filled their plastic drinking cups with water from the spigot by the porch and spritzed it at each other just enough so the teacher wouldn't notice.

Lizzie's favorite phrase was "Oh, good grief," which was funny, the way she rolled her eyes. Annie and Fannie weren't allowed to say it at home, because Mam said it was a worldly form of expression. They said it whenever they were out of earshot, though.

They were seated according to age, the ten-year-olds coming last, or almost. The age to leave your mother's side on the wooden bench was nine, so the twins had only been *mitt die maid nei gay* (going in with the girls) for a bit over a year. Nine was the age where you were considered old enough to sit quietly away from your mother for three hours and behave. They might not appear unruly, but in their hearts, they actually were. They folded their small handkerchiefs into a deft trick of making two "babies" appear in a cradle, then held them the way a real baby was held and rocked back and forth, causing suppressed giggles up and down the row of girls. Or they loosened straight pins from their belts and scratched their arms, creating their initials in small scabs, kind of like a tattoo but not nearly as bad.

Mam could not see them, the way she was seated facing the ministers and the older men. They sat a few rows behind the women, which was nice. When they knelt to pray, though, Mam had a bird's-eye view of their behavior, so they didn't dare whisper or make dolls in cradles out of their handkerchiefs but stayed on their knees for the long German prayer and barely twitched a muscle.

The older girls always filed out to use the restroom after the first short prayer, when the deacon read Scripture, a practice seemingly long standing, but discouraged by the ministry at times. The congregation stood to hear Scripture reading, so it was easier to slip out unnoticed. Sometimes they both went out, and sometimes only one of them, which Mam would accept for a while, until they became bold and both of them went every Sunday, and Mam would crack down on them, saying it was not necessary to go to the restroom every time.

They tried to focus on the sermon, but there were many distractions. Children became fussy, babies cried, fathers got up to hand a crying infant to its mother. Dogs barked, or traffic moved past a window. Mam said where she came from, in Pennsylvania, they used to hand a tray of moon pies around for the little ones halfway through the service. Moon pies were crescents of pie crust filled with dried apple filling, or *schnitz*, a little pie to hold in your hand. But here in Kentucky, they all came from the eastern or Lancaster people, so no one ever handed a delicious snack to anyone. You simply sat there and endured to the end.

Annie sighed, straightened her back, sniffed, and coughed. Her nose felt clogged, so she unfolded her small flowered handkerchief and blew into it. After sniffing again, she realized it hadn't been sufficient so applied the handkerchief again and snorted more vigorously. The noises coming from her sister sent a deep shame through Fannie, so she sent a well-directed elbow into her side, hitting squarely in Annie's ticklish rib area. She exhaled sharply, over-reacted, and fell completely off the bench with a loud clatter. Heads turned, registering alarm.

Who had fallen off the bench?

Quickly, Annie lifted herself from the floor, her face flaming. She bowed her head. Fannie bowed hers. They both wished the floor could open up and swallow them, but what actually happened was even worse. Footsteps, then Mam's dark form with outstretched arm, and both girls were taken to sit on the bench with her, the ultimate humiliation for anyone not seated with a parent. Annie's face felt scorched and she blinked back quick tears. Fannie looked at the floor for so long, Annie was afraid there was something wrong with her neck. But the worst part was waiting for the silent pinch that was sure to come, which of course, was applied in due time.

A firm grasp of the flesh on their forearms, a bit of pressure, and a hard squeeze from Mam's thumb and forefinger. They winced, accepted the punishment, and sat quietly as the pain subsided.

Annie daydreamed, allowed her imagination to run wild. What if the floor *had* opened, and she'd gone down the rabbit hole like Alice in Wonderland? She imagined being taken to a nice cozy room with a couch in it and pillows with soft throws and a rug. A nice lady would serve moon pies and pretzels with soft cheese and all the lemonade they could drink. Or Pepsi or hot chocolate with marshmallows and whipped cream. Not Cool Whip, but that stuff in a squirt can to make fancy designs all over pancakes or cupcakes. And she could lie back on the pillows and read Laura Ingalls Wilder books, covered cozily with a pink fleece throw.

By the time church was over, the last song sung, she'd forgotten about falling off the bench, for the most part. Becky and Sarah were too polite to mention it, and they helped hold babies and watch the two-year-olds while the mothers ate. It was their duty and one they always enjoyed, or at least Fannie did. Annie wasn't too crazy about babies, especially the ones that slobbered all over their soaking wet bibs and grabbed your covering strings until it tugged horribly on the pins imbedded in your hair. Babies were heavy and squirmed on your lap, and sometimes they bit you when you were least prepared, chomped down on your arm or finger like a dog. It hurt a lot.

She liked holding the newborns best, because they simply lay swaddled in blankets with their eyes closed most of the time. When they began to move around and grimace, she'd hand the baby off to Fannie.

When the girls were finally ushered to the table, they sat waiting until every available seat was full, then bowed their heads to say the silent prayer. As they grasped their knives to spread cup cheese on a slice of homemade bread, someone from behind asked if they wanted coffee, which was strictly forbidden by Mam (she said it would stunt their growth). They drank water, ate cheese spread on their bread, red beets, small slices of pickle, and schnitz pie. It was very good, a light, traditional lunch served at every church service. Sometimes there was ham or other lunch meat or red beet eggs, but today there was neither, so they ate what was set on the table and were satisfied.

After they ate, they went to the house and talked with their friends, played with babies, or explored the house, until Mam came to tell them Dat was ready to go. Shawls and bonnets on, they were bundled back into the buggy. This time there was no grumbling from Ruth and Naomi, who didn't care about their aprons being crushed now that they were headed home.

No one mentioned the unspeakable until Naomi asked pointedly why Annie slid off the bench.

"Hush, Naomi. The girls had their punishment."

Dat nodded in agreement, which was so kind-hearted a lump rose in each of their throats, and they almost cried.

The horse trotted briskly, the colorful leaves tumbling onto the road and covering the forest floors and edges of pastureland. Pine trees swayed in the stiff breeze and the horse's mane and tail blew up and out as Dat reached up to close the window against the cold. Naomi reached over for a section of Annie's shawl to cover her lap, but she grabbed it away, having not the slightest sisterly love for her or Ruth.

But when they arrived home, the twins were happy to shed their shawls and bonnets, capes and aprons, head coverings and shoes, and change into short-sleeved everyday dresses and their house slippers. They went to the kitchen for a snack, in spite of having eaten at church. There was pumpkin pie and Naomi made a popperful of popcorn, which was enticing until she seasoned it with every spice she could possibly think of, ruining it completely. Fannie made another batch, with browned butter and salt, which was much better. They had cold cider to drink.

They played Sorry and Uno, but were not allowed to play Monopoly on Sunday because it involved money, and spending money on the Lord's Day was forbidden. Mam fell asleep on the recliner, her mouth dropping open and soft snores coming from her nose. Dat read the *Family Life* on the couch until he drifted off and the *Family Life* fell on the rug beside him.

After a while, Mike came down to the kitchen, then Amos, who each poured a glass of cider and filled a bowl with popcorn. They peered over the girls' shoulders, watching the Uno game. The big girls—*die groszie maid*—were all at their friends' houses, which was a good thing. It was nice having them always gone on Sunday afternoon. Mike and Amos had girlfriends now, which was also a blessing, the way they left earlier to pick them up to go to the supper for the youth. Ephraim and John roamed the countryside on Sunday afternoons, their only time to explore, find deer or foxes, raccoon homes high in the trees, or groundhog holes and ring-necked pheasant sightings.

Ruth and Naomi became bored with the Uno game, due to the fact that neither one was winning, and wandered off. Annie and Fannie begged them to stay, but it did no good, so they put the games away, cleaned the tabletop, and swept the floor before donning thick sweaters and scarves and going outside to ride their scooters.

"Uh-oh," Fannie muttered as she wheeled her purple scooter from the shed. "Flat tire."

"Use Ephraim's."

"I could, but what if he comes back?"

"He won't."

They were wheeling it from the shed when Mike came out to get his horse ready to hitch to the buggy. He was all dressed up, although his face looked older, too old to be without a beard.

"Hey. You could put air in Fannie's scooter," Annie said.

"Sure. Bring it over to the air hose."

He squatted to unscrew the cap on the tire, applied the nozzle, and pressed, putting air into the flaccid tire.

"You sure there's no hole in it?" he asked.

"I doubt it. It's been wobbly for a while."

"There you go."

"Thanks, Mike."

They pushed their scooters out the gravel drive-way and walked them up the first big hill, around a curve and up another long hill, then turned around and headed back down, careful to stay inside the white line on the shoulder of the macadam road.

The cold air hit their faces as they picked up speed, but they did not place their heels on the foot-brakes at all, simply held steady to the handlebars and whizzed down the hills, then walked all the way back up to enjoy the ride all over again. Then they pushed back home again, flung their scooters in the shed, and went to the barn, watched the horses munching loose bits of hay, and wished for a pony, the way they always did.

Dat and Mam were overprotective, in their opinion. They had never allowed the girls to drive a pony by themselves unless an older brother was available to accompany them. It had all happened the day Blaze, a black, feisty, high-stepping Hackney pony, spooked at a flapping canvas on a produce truck, ran up over a steep embankment, and dumped Mary and Salome by the side of the road, breaking Salome's arm high up, close to the shoulder, which required surgery and a very large hospital fee. A few months later, ironically, the same thing happened again, except it was down an embankment and it wasn't a produce truck, but a rattling steel-wheeled tractor driven by a neighbor who was a Mennonite. No fault of his, certainly, and he was kind enough to stop the tractor and help Becky, whose foot had been crushed by the cart when it upset.

"Enough is enough," Dat said, and the pony and cart were sold, with Mam nodding her head in solid support.

"But, Dat, a Shetland pony is different," they said.

"No," Mam said. "Absolutely not."

"What about a miniature pony, then?"

"Too small, too expensive."

So they rode their scooters and wished for a pony. From time to time, they reminded their parents about Benny Stoltzfus driving his Shetland pony to school every day, and he was their age. *Every day*, they pointed out. That was the reason the pony was so well behaved. He was driven every day, and with Blaze, it was only once a week, if that. Amos said the girls had a point, but in the end, Mam ruled, saying no pony was safe, they were all contrary, strong-willed little horses, and she would have none of it.

They fed the calves, then went to the cow stable to watch the cows being milked, hoping to catch Dat in a jovial mood, the way he usually was on a Sunday evening after a good nap. He was singing, which was a good sign.

"There you are," he sang out. "Calves fed?"

"Sure are."

"Good. I can always depend on you."

They smiled, and he smiled back.

After a while, Fannie nodded at Annie, and Annie put her hands behind her back and asked, "Dat, don't you ever think about getting a pony?

"Now why would I do something like that?"

"Well . . . we thought maybe you'd change your mind."

"After those two accidents? I think not."

"But we're old enough to train a pony now. We could work with it every day."

"Now come on, girls. You know your mother will never give in. That was very hard for her, seeing those two accidents. I don't think we'll risk it again."

They sighed as loudly as they could. They hoped they appeared sad and pathetic, completely forlorn. They sat on the curb of the concrete feed trough side by side, their shoulders slumped, their chins in their hands, but as far as they could tell, this had no effect on Dat. He went right on changing milkers and singing. More like bellowing, really.

"Will the circle be unbroken, by and by? Lord, by and by?"

It was irritating, his lack of caring.

Finally, they got to their feet, wandered back into the house, hung up their sweaters and scarves, and sat at the kitchen table to try out their sad countenances on Mam. She was also in a good mood, humming low under her breath as she fried onions and green peppers in a high-walled cast iron skillet, completely absorbed in her work and never glancing their way.

Chapter Four

ON MONDAY AS THEY WALKED TO SCHOOL, the twins were quiet and subdued as Naomi and Ruth chattered away about the upcoming Christmas play. Ruth was sure she'd be chosen to lead in one of the best parts, the way her voice carried so well, and Naomi planned on singing a special song. Annie and Fannie walked a few steps behind them, amazed at their confidence, even a bit in awe of them.

Christmas programs weren't easy.

For one thing, the smaller pupils were never given the best parts, especially if you were shy or if your voice was high pitched and didn't carry very well. Neither of them had ever been in a play but had no reason to believe they wouldn't be in one this year, being in fourth grade and at the top of their class.

Fannie shivered, the cold air sending chills up her spine. Annie shivered, too, then wished the girls would be quiet, would not talk about scary subjects on the way to school. Well, Thanksgiving wasn't here yet, and no Christmas program parts were handed out until that day arrived, so they could enjoy a few weeks of not knowing for sure.

Behind them, there was the distinct sound of tripping little hooves. They lifted hands in greeting and stood in awe as Benny Stoltzfus and his little sister rode past, the Shetland pony perfectly behaved, the little hooves pattering on the macadam as he trotted by.

They sighed and walked on.

It wasn't fair, really. Here was the most adorable pony they had ever seen, black and white paint, his thick black mane and tail gleaming in the sun, the black cart etched with gold designs, the seat upholstered to match. It wasn't the twins' fault there had been two accidents. Dat could blame himself, buying that high-stepping Hackney, who was never trained to obey properly, especially after the first accident when he dumped the girls off.

But when they arrived at school, they went inside to set their lunchboxes on the shelf and say good morning to Teacher Rachel, who still greeted them with a disarming sniff as she had every morning since the rubber-band-shooting incident.

There was still time for a bit of baseball before the first bell. The boys were grouped around home plate, having a heated conversation about the upcoming horse and pony sale at the local auction barn, held in the late fall for the plain community. Benny Stoltzfus considered himself an expert, driving that pony to school, so he was saying there were a great many horses and likely as many ponies. Harvey Troyer was bringing quite a few good horses, and Ben Weaver, too. Annie and Fannie stood on the sidelines without a word, but they realized how very much they wanted to go.

All day, their minds kept drifting off, spinning with new possibilities, the ways in which they could present their case to their parents. There was no use getting an okay from Dat if Mam wouldn't give her consent, that was sure. No matter how submissive Mam appeared to be, she knew exactly how to control Dat, and that was the truth.

"Fannie?"

She jumped. What was the question?

Teacher Rachel frowned, said it would be nice if she paid attention. Did she know the golden rule?

Quickly, she recited it expertly. Of course she knew it. They had learned it in first grade.

"Very good. Annie?"

Annie repeated it.

All day, the thought stayed with them. The golden rule would be a good approach. "Do unto others as you would have them do to you." If Dat and Mam took this seriously enough, surely they could see that the right thing to do was to give their children a pony.

They discussed this at length on the way home, stopping to pick up a handful of acorns to take off the caps and peel them. They tasted them repeatedly, found them disgusting, but kept trying, thinking the next one might be better, which it never was.

"Squirrels like them," Annie offered.

"We aren't squirrels."

"Deer eat them. Ephraim says they love acorns."

"We aren't deer either. Wish we were. Annie, I want a pony so bad, and Dat just can't see it. I don't want to wait till I'm married to be able to drive a pony."

"I know, I know. We're going to keep asking."

"Both of us, right?"

"Both of us."

* * *

The house was warm, the windows steamed up, the double burner canner bubbling away on the gas stove. Mam was canning neck pumpkins for pumpkin pie, pumpkin bars, and cookies, delicious items everyone loved. It was hard work, peeling those neck pumpkins, but Mam said no store-bought pumpkin from a can could compare. So, with the pony on their minds, they decided the best way to Mam's heart was offering to peel pumpkins.

"No, no, you're not strong enough. Salome is here and Ruth and Naomi. Besides, we're almost done."

"Well, what can we do?"

Mam laid down her paring knife, suddenly paying attention to the earnest pleading look on her two daughters' faces, then sat down with a weary sigh.

"Alright, tell me what's on your mind. You don't ordinarily come home from school and offer to work. Tell me."

Annie looked at Fannie. Fannie looked at her. They gave a little nod.

"Well, it's just this way. We don't think it's fair that we can't have a pony. It is not our fault Dat bought a Hackney." Fannie spoke with a heavy emphasis on her father's choice of ponies.

Annie took up the cause, saying a Shetland pony was a far wiser choice, and did she think it was fair to deprive them of the pleasure of driving a pony? Huh, did she?

Mam shook her head and made a funny clucking sound, as if she was sucking on her teeth.

"Alright, girls. I'll tell you exactly how it is. God was clearly sending a warning by allowing those two accidents, and we must accept it. No, I can never, with a free conscience, allow you two to drive a pony on the road. What if we did allow it, and one or both of you were killed? I could never forgive myself for having not heeded God's warning."

"But, Mam, Benny Stoltzfus . . ."

Mam held up a hand.

"Is only a year older," Fannie finished.

"No."

They went upstairs very slowly, laid side by side, their backs to each other, and cried soft little whimpers that came up from the despair of their hearts. They hadn't even had a chance to bring up the golden rule. After a while, Annie went to the bathroom across the hall and rolled a wad of bathroom tissue in her hand, went back, and handed half to her sister. They both blew their noses, sat, and stared bleakly out the window. They watched a brown leaf twist and turn on its stem, the November wind tossing it around and around.

"We have to give up," Annie said miserably.

"We haven't tried Dat yet . . . at least not today," Fannie said hopefully.

So they did just that. They waited until chores were over and he'd taken off his shoes. He sat back in his chair at the kitchen table, hooked his finger through the handle of his mug of tea, and watched them, seated opposite him on the bench.

"Dat?"

"Yes?"

"Are you going to the horse sale in two weeks?"

"What horse sale?"

"Benny Stoltfuz was saying there will be a huge sale."

"I didn't know that."

"Well, we think it's not fair that we aren't allowed to have a pony."

Up went only one of Dat's eyebrows. Down went his mug of tea. He extended his forefinger and scratched his ear. He blinked. He cleared his throat and coughed.

Mam took the last jar of pumpkin from the canner, tightened the lid with a quick twist of her wrist, hung up the dish towel and turned, leaned against the counter, and crossed her arms. She wasn't glaring exactly, but she wasn't smiling either.

"Does Mam know anything about this?"

Guilty eyes flew to their mother's unflinching gaze.

"Yes."

"And what did she say?"

"I don't want to say it," Annie said weakly.

"I know, Annie. I know how she feels. And I must say I feel the same. Maybe not as strongly, but surely you are old enough to realize our concerns."

"But it's not fair."

"I'll tell you what. If there's a horse sale coming up, why don't we go? Is it on a Saturday?"

"I think so."

"So we'll go. Not to buy a pony, but just to introduce you to the great big world of horse sales. Mam, do you want to go?"

"No, no. That's not up my alley at all. But the girls can go."

Dat turned to the door of the living room, asking Ruth and Naomi, who agreed to go, eagerly.

Fannie rolled her eyes at Annie and vice versa. So much for a pony, with those two holding court. But there was always a sliver of hope, a tiny ray of *maybe this was still possible*, in spite of the obstacles.

After everyone was in bed, Dat approached Mam, asking for her honest opinion. Mam thought for a long time, but finally told him she simply couldn't get past the image in her mind of that twisted pony cart and Salome's pain and terror. Ponies were trouble, they weren't trustworthy. Why risk it again?

"I know you're right. But is it really fair to the twins?"

"I don't know."

"I was thinking about a small riding horse. A quarterhorse, or a Morgan."

"That might be OK. Just one or one for each of them?"

"Maybe one for each. Riding a good horse in the fields doesn't seem as risky, as long as they stay off the road away from traffic. You know how strong and athletic they both are. I believe they'd be great riders, eventually."

"Yes. Anything to keep them off the road." Mam nodded her head, her brow knitted.

"I'll take them to the sale, watch their reaction to the riders, talk to a few dealers. Why don't we surprise them for Christmas?"

"Would that be fair to the rest of the family?" Mam asked, raising a concern he hadn't thought of.

"I'll bring any of the children who are interested," Dat said, quickly solving the problem. "

Mam worried about her girls, how unladylike riding would be. None of the girls had ever ridden a horse.

"None of them have ever been like the twins, either," reminded Dat.

"That is so true. Well, we'll figure something out. They'll have to wear trousers of some kind."

And so they agreed on a plan but kept it between the two of them.

Fannie told Annie she could see no hope for owning a pony, but perhaps they should be happy just to go to the sale.

"Why?" Annie asked. "It's like being on a diet and going to a bake sale. Why watch all those cute ponies when we know it's impossible to own one?"

"We'll have to ask Benny to give us a ride."

"I'm not asking Benny."

"Okay, then I will."

* * *

The day of the sale was one of those early November days when the sky is slate gray, heavy with cold rain, an ominous wind churning the undersides of lowering clouds, bare branches rattling against window panes, and a few stubborn leaves clinging to heaving limbs. Heavy frost had turned the pastures a dull green and brown, weeds a dismal frostbitten gray, the earth cold and damp as it awaited the onslaught of frigid winter temperatures.

Mam put more wood on the fire in the kitchen that morning and held her hands to the warmth as shivers raced up her spine. She looked up to find the twins peeping around the staircase, up at six o'clock, ready to have their hair combed and belt aprons pinned in place.

"Well, good morning," she said, smiling.

"Good morning, Mam."

As she did their hair, she told them gently to accept their decision, and to be good girls.

"To be denied something we really want is never easy, but it's very good for the soul. Someday you'll understand."

That all sounded terribly depressing, like the end of the world would be coming that day, so they didn't bother answering. What Mam said made absolutely

no sense. They wanted a pony. How was it good for
their souls not to get one?

They wore heavy coats, but Mam said it was okay
to leave their bonnets at home, the way they ham-
pered your hearing. Ruth and Naomi decided not to
come that morning after a quick dash to the window,
hearing the branches thrashing about in the wind,
the cold slapping their faces. Annie and Fannie tried
to conceal their happiness, but their eyes were shining when they left.

They felt so grown up, seated on the front seat. It
was Mam's rightful place, but today, it was all theirs.
They sat tightly side by side, as straight as possible,
and spoke with as much respect as they could. Dat
commented on the lack of a bonnets, then grinned
when they told him about Mam's theory of a bonnet
at a horse sale.

"Like blinders on a bridle, huh?" he asked.

They nodded happily. Dat wasn't as strict as
Mam, as far as *ordnung* went. She was always worried
about offending someone, or simply abusing her own
ideas of what was wrong and what was right. She
didn't like to think of her children wanting to follow

the latest styles, had no desire to sew clothes she felt were inappropriate. Perfectly happy to stay within the *ordnung*, she hoped to instill this virtue into each of her many sons and daughters. If any of them worried her, it was Annie and Fannie, always searching for the next step up to another trail of excitement. Why couldn't they be satisfied to be ordinary little girls who played with dolls and tea sets?

They had never been like the other girls. A small tin tea set she had given them years ago, white with pink roses painted on every piece, had never been used. She thought it might still be in the original box, perhaps Christmas wrapping and pieces of tape still clinging to it. Dolls were cast aside; their small play table used for building blocks or crayons and coloring books. They kept a whole posse of barn cats, rescued turtles and frogs, ran after groundhogs. She loved them dearly, but worried that their wild hearts would get them in danger or lead them astray as they got older.

Mam sighed and began her Saturday baking.

* * *

The sale barn was a gleaming white, low building set against a backdrop of trees, the dark sky behind them creating a picturesque scene. Vehicles, trucks, horse trailers, horses, a colorful array of coats, bill caps, black Amish hats, and narrow-brimmed gray Mennonite hats all created a pleasant atmosphere of excitement as they drove around the outside of the ring to stable their own horse. They had never seen a horse run as fast or with his neck arched as high or his forelegs lifted like the one in the ring. Speechless, they climbed off the buggy and turned to stare, barely able to breathe. It was almost more than they could comprehend, the beauty and grace of these fine, gleaming black or brown horses.

Dat took one of each of their hands until they found a spot where they could watch the driving horses. The twins peeked between coats of bystanders, completely thrilled. A girl rode out on a golden-yellow horse with an almost white mane and tail. She wasn't very old, perhaps only a few years older than themselves. The horse pranced sideways, then forward, shook his head and pulled on the reins, but she remained seated, calm as could be. And she was Amish.

This took their breath away. Her covering was pinned securely, her black coat buttoned, her skirts modestly wide enough to be below the knee, although there was a length of what appeared to be trousers, or at least stretchy pants of some sort. And she wore boots, real cowboy boots that weren't too ornate, sort of plain, which was appropriate for Amish people.

Elbows were quickly jammed into each other's sides.

"She's Amish!" hissed Annie.

"She's riding a wild horse!" Fannie breathed.

"Not wild. Just excited."

"But look! Watch how she rides. She's stuck like glue."

"Oh. Oh, my goodness. Look!"

Neither could not take their eyes off the golden horse and its rider. She had loosened the reins only a bit, which was the signal the horse had been waiting on, instantly lowering his haunches and digging in, taking off into the wind in a graceful, lilting gallop, the mane and tail lifting in a pale stream. The golden horse gathered his legs beneath him and picked up speed as he leaned into the curve, the girl leaning perfectly, as if she was a part of the beautiful animal.

Another rider appeared, then another, but neither one could compete. Their arms flapped, they slid around awkwardly in the saddle, but were unaware of their own clumsiness as they rounded the circle. But the twins were aware. That day, they were fully woken to the fact of how much they wanted to be that girl on a horse. Forget a pony and cart.

Annie tugged on Dat's coat, looked imploringly into his lowered gaze. "If you don't want to buy a pony, we could learn to ride a horse in the pasture. Like she does. That would be safer, right?"

"Horses are very expensive."

But he was smiling, which was a good sign. More elbowing instantly took place. They shivered with excitement and cold, but were hardly able to go inside when Dat was ready.

Inside the large building, another surprise awaited them. Seats like benches were stacked in rising tiers along each wall. Everywhere they looked, people were filing in, finding seats so that everyone could see above everyone else. It was amazing, how someone had been smart enough to think of this.

A constant stream of horses and ponies were led into the small enclosed area, with the auctioneer and his helpers housed in a sort of pedestal, with a microphone placed in front of him. His voice was magnified ten times, coming from boxes hung in the corner, which was fascinating. But the horses were the true wonder.

Both of the girls had eyes only for the riding horses, but tried to remember that Dat would probably never buy one for them. They tried to think perhaps, just perhaps, he would consider it someday, but when they saw him visiting with the man beside him, not even watching the horses, their hopes were dashed.

Well, they'd take what they could get. If they were allowed to come to a horse sale occasionally, at least that was something. This was whispered to each other, with a deep understanding and a sense of total agreement.

Chapter Five

THEY WALKED TO SCHOOL ON MONDAY morning, placed squarely back to earth, their feet scuffling along the macadam as they swung their lunchboxes in rhythm to their steps.

"Well, you talk about Mike and his 'Christmas every day,'" Annie remarked. "Can you even imagine how great Christmas Day would be if we got a riding horse?"

Fannie eyed her sourly. "Don't even try to imagine it."

"I'm just saying how nice that would be."

"Speaking of Mike, he hasn't been acting like it's Christmas every day. Guess he isn't as happy as he thought he'd be."

"Guess not."

"Well, if Dat bought us a riding horse, I can absolutely say we would never get tired of it. We'd keep learning and just get better and better. Right?"

"For sure."

* * *

Buoyed by hopes of a riding horse, nothing seemed impossible as Teacher Rachel handed out parts for the Christmas plays. Annie caught her lower lip, bowed her head over her papers, and scowled. Every one of her lines was highlighted in yellow, and there were three pages of dialogue. All those yellow words were hers.

She looked over at Fannie, who sat still as stone, staring at her own sheaf of papers. She mouthed, "Look at mine," then looked away quickly.

Pupils raised their hands, asked questions, some of them looking perplexed, some of them anxious, others grinning excitedly. Teacher Rachel spoke of songs to be sung, the afternoons of practice, and all the artwork still to be done. When school was dismissed, there was a general hubbub as pupils compared play parts, shared copies of poems, and shrieked or lamented or complained.

The twins walked home from school aware of the hard work of memorizing all those lines, their somber mood matching the lowering skies. The only thing they had to look forward to was Thanksgiving Day, with all the food and family and fun. All the siblings would be there for dinner, of course, and maybe the new girlfriends.

Dat and Mam liked to keep old ways, lamenting the fact of losing the *schaum und tzucht*, that bashful, hidden away kind of dating, the way their forefathers had done it. Often, dating couples did not even meet either set of parents until the couple was engaged or close to it, but nowadays, they were introduced early on. Mam disapproved of the new ways. Dating should be kept private, she thought, quiet and humble, in keeping with Amish tradition.

Mam never served a whole turkey the way English folks did in pictures, but instead baked the whole beautiful thing during the night, then tore it all apart with a knife and kitchen scissors, creating little pieces of meat she mixed with bread cubes and lots of celery cooked in butter, then baked it all together to make *roascht*. It was delicious with mashed potatoes and gravy. But still, Fannie especially lamented the lack of a whole turkey baked to a golden brown with fancy parsley and grapes around it. Mam was just too committed to tradition and the old ways, and she would probably never change.

When they arrived home from school, Mam's face was pink with the heat from the oven, her pumpkin pies ready to be taken out, the tops a perfect golden color, the countertop arrayed with fruit for the girls to cut for fruit salad. She greeted them a bit absent-mindedly, so they knew preparations were in full swing. Fannie started on the apples, bossy as always, instructing Annie to get started on the oranges. Annie looked at the huge navel oranges, knew the peels were far too thick and heavy for her, and picked up the cellophane bag of purple grapes.

"Annie, I said oranges."

"Grapes are easier."

"Mam?"

"Girls, I don't have time to straighten up your silliness. Annie, do the oranges. Ruth, you and Naomi get started cleaning the upstairs before milking time. Hurry up."

When Mam wasn't watching, Annie grabbed Fannie's forearm between her thumb and forefinger, giving the loose skin a satisfying twist. Fannie yelped, grabbed Annie's arm, and hung on. The scuffle ended when they dissolved in a fit of giggles, and because Annie knew she was outnumbered, she picked up an orange and a paring knife and looked from one to the other, before biting her tongue and getting to work.

"Leave the apple peels on," Mam instructed Fannie. "It gives the fruit salad a nice color."

Mam was whipping caramel frosting for the chocolate layer cake, which would be served with a huge bowl of vanilla pudding she stirred on the stove for a long time. She also made pecan pie and blueberry crumble pie, but never Annie's favorite for Thanksgiving Day, chocolate shoofly pie. Mam said chocolate shoofly was too much like chocolate cake, and besides, three kinds of pie was enough.

There was only bean soup for supper that night. Well, and red beet eggs, dill pickles, and homemade sweet bologna. No one asked for dessert, knowing they'd be refused.

"Why would someone even think of making bean soup?" Annie asked as they filled pails of warm water in the milkhouse sink.

"It's quick. Mam's busy."

"So?"

"I guess you're right. There is canned vegetable soup in the basement."

"And chicken corn soup."

Fannie lifted the plastic bucket up over the front of the sink, added an empty one, and looked, really looked, at her sister.

"You know we're supposed to be grateful for everything set before us."

"Well, I wasn't. Bean soup is disgusting."

"Red beet eggs are worse. Totally worse."

"We'll eat tomorrow. Can't wait."

They were up early, fed the calves and swept the forebay before a quick breakfast of scrambled eggs and toast. The house was spotless, windows gleaming in the morning light, the bathroom smelling of floor cleaner and soap. They wore school dresses and black aprons, their hair brought into submission by the spritz bottle of water and the fine-toothed comb. Naomi and Ruth peeled potatoes after the breakfast dishes were washed, dried, and put away.

Mike and Amos slept until eight o'clock, came down to the kitchen disheveled and resigned to their fate of cold cereal. Any latecomers would be expected to look out for themselves on holidays, so the corn flakes and Honey Nut Cheerios boxes soon adorned the table.

"Hurry, hurry," Mam sang out. "I need time to set the table."

Mike good-naturedly gave her a wide smile, and Amos pointed to the clock, said it wasn't anywhere near dinnertime.

Mike appeared to be a bit nervous, and Amos kept rolling his eyes, pointing at Mam, raising eyebrows, so Fannie and Annie looked at each other, decided silently it would be fun to hang around, see what they had up their sleeves.

When Mike cleared his throat, they stood stock still, their eyes and ears wide open.

"Mam, we asked Miriam and Sadie to come for Thanksgiving dinner, if that's okay."

Mam stood very still, her back turned.

"You see, things are done a bit differently now," Mike ventured.

Ma turned. "Does Dat know?"

"Yes. We asked. He said I should ask you if it's alright."

Mam pursed her lips, inhaled, then let her shoulders droop, the first sign of resignation. "Well, if he said so, then I'll have to give myself up." She paused, clearly battling with her own will. "But just so you know, it wasn't always this way. I would never have asked my mother to bring Dat to the family Thanksgiving dinner."

"He said that."

"He did? Well, good. You know I like to keep things the way the forefathers taught us. I guess I'm a real traditionalist, is what I am. But some of these old ways are worth keeping. You know how Isaac was led by God to travel to a faraway land to find a wife, the beautiful Rebecca, who covered her face with her mantle when she saw him. That was so beautiful, that clear picture of a humble bride. So old-fashioned and precious. Here we are, acting like worldly people, bringing their girlfriends to Thanksgiving."

"Oh, come on, Mam. That's insulting. Don't you want to meet the girlfriends?"

"No, not really." Her voice was stern, her face lined with worry. Her dedication to tradition was stronger than her concern for her boys' views.

"Well, I'm sorry, but we invited them. Dat is okay with it, and it is what it is."

Amos spoke with kindness, but also with a firm undertone that grabbed Mam's attention. He was no longer a boy, but a full-grown man. Yet he was still her son and should show her respect.

She could think of no suitable reply, so she set her lips in a line and added two more plates to the stack to be set around the table.

* * *

She was elbow deep in the steaming kettle of cooked potatoes, wielding the potato masher with unparalleled fury, when the laundry room door opened and Mike ushered Miriam into the kitchen, followed by Amos and Sadie.

"Mam?"

She stopped, turned, her eyes taking in the two girls, both dressed in identical fall colors. Without capes. Her lips twitched. Slowly, she reached for the dishrag and wiped her hands before a smile reached her mouth. It was a small smile, one that didn't quite reach the whole way across, but it was a smile.

"Mam, this is Miriam Stoltzfus. Miriam, my mother."

Much to her credit, a blush spread across Miriam's face as she looked full into Mam's eyes, offered a hand, and Mam took it.

"Hello."

"Nice to meet you."

The greeting was repeated for Sadie, who was shorter and had darker hair and eyes. There was no blush, only a frank, appraising look, but her smile was genuine, warm. Both girls were no longer young, so there was a certain air of sophistication, like a rose in full bloom, as if they'd grown into knowing who they were.

"Do you need help mashing potatoes?" Sadie asked, her voice low, the words plainly spoken.

Quickly, Mam refused her help, said the girls were able, so the boys asked if they wanted to sit in the living room a while. Miriam appeared to be grateful, like a rescued puppy, Fannie said later.

The big girls—Sarah, Becky, Salome, and Mary—knew Sadie and Miriam, greeted them warmly, then returned to their duties. Salome was arranging asters in a vase filled with water, Mary lighting pumpkin spice candles. The big girls had persuaded Mam to add a special touch, just once, for Miriam and Sadie. Mam had given her signature snort, but relented, even producing a Yankee Candle for the bathroom and allowing the twins to light it.

So they felt very classy indeed, standing in the bathroom with its white walls and fixtures, the basket of ivy and the sign that said SEIZE THE DAY! Mam was not about to put Bible verses or God's name up on the walls, saying Christianity was to be practiced, letting your light shine with good works and not plastered all over your walls. Evidently, there was nothing wrong with "Seize the day!"—although the girls thought the bathroom was rather an odd place for the statement.

Mam had outdone herself with her cooking, though. The humble platter of *roascht* was steaming hot with tender chunks of white meat and celery in clumps of buttery, toasted bread, the gravy was thick and savory, the potatoes fluffy and full of sour cream and butter with more browned butter running down the sides. There were wide, thick noodles, broccoli steamed to perfection, peas and carrots, and a sweet potato casserole with a crunchy nut topping.

There was one dish neither Annie nor Fannie would touch. Scalloped oysters. They were positively sick. Wet and salty and slimy. They smelled. Dat dug in with a big spoon and thumped a large quivering mess on his plate, drawing a collective *E-ew-ew* from the twins. He laughed, said they tasted like the ocean, citing the fact that he'd actually been to the ocean quite a few times in his youth.

Dat had never been as conservative as Mam, this they knew. He sowed quite a few wild oats before "settling down" with the gentle Malinda Fisher, a distant cousin from *die una Beckvay*—the southern part of Lancaster County, which was known to be lived at a quieter, more old-fashioned pace. Plain, shy, but with a very pretty face and a graceful walk, he'd fallen hard, won her hand, and had never regretted his choice.

Annie thought Miriam was prettiest, but Fannie liked Sadie's snappy style. They both agreed the girlfriends were pretty fancy, without a cape and their dresses sewed up the front, instead of snaps on the outside. Plus, their dresses were long. Miriam's almost touched the floor.

("My oh," Mam said later, sadly. "My oh. It doesn't bide well for the next of kin." But she only said it to Salome and Mary, not to the twins.)

The dinner was quite jolly though, on Dat's part. He tried to keep the conversation lively, making comical remarks about various subjects, his eyes sliding sideways to Mam, as if checking to make sure she was approving of his style of entertainment. Everyone knew if Mam approved, everything would come up roses, and if she didn't, you had quite a few prickly thorns to contend with.

The pumpkin pie was perfect, the custard rich and creamy, the crust flaky and sweet. But the best part of the whole meal was the chocolate layer cake with thick pudding piled over the top, a side of fruit salad to balance the chocolate.

Mam waved away the compliments, but drank her coffee with crinkles along her eyes, meaning she was pleased. She exchanged a look with Dat, and all was well for Fannie and Annie, their stomachs full and the atmosphere pleasant, in spite of the girlfriends.

Everyone helped with the dishes afterward, which seemed to pile up in alarming amounts. There were no paper plates and certainly no plastic utensils or cups. Mam viewed all that as a genuine waste of money, and only for women too lazy to wash dishes. Her collection of Corelle plates was impressive, items found in thrift stores and yard sales, all white with no design.

Sarah wiped plates and unkindly hustled Annie and Fannie out of the kitchen. It wasn't that they were eager to help, but they didn't appreciate her being so short with them. They moved to the living room and told each other she was just mad she couldn't invite a boyfriend to Thanksgiving dinner and that she was, for real, getting to be an old grouch. They said it was no wonder she didn't have a boyfriend, you could see she wasn't sweet or kind.

They all assembled in the spacious living room with three couches and three matching recliners, a large braided rug, and two propane lamps with white shades set in a cabinet. There was a family record on the wall with Dat's parents and all his siblings, birthdates, and everything. And one with Mam's family.

Dat handed out the German songbooks, then took his place on the recliner, beside Mam. Annie and Fannie scrambled to perch on either side of him, on the wide arms of his chair, eagerly waiting till he announced the first song. They loved to sing with Dat, his deep baritone melding with their own high voices, the older boys singing tenor, and Becky and Sarah adding the alto. Mam sang a sweet soprano, and when everyone chimed in, it was, in fact, a little part of Heaven in their house.

They watched to see if Miriam and Sadie could sing and were relieved to see they enjoyed it. Or seemed to. Miriam sat beside Mike, very close actually, and Sadie was squeezed in beside Amos on the same couch, which was very tight.

After the singing was over, they all went outside in the cold, set up bases in the pasture, and played a lively game of baseball while Mam and Dat lay back in their recliners and rested their eyes.

Annie and Fannie weren't allowed to play ball, which was a bit insulting, but mostly it was okay. After all, they did not want to strike out with Miriam and Sadie watching.

It was one of the best Thanksgiving days ever, they agreed. Just a great day spent with family and good food, good songs, and the excitement of the new girlfriends.

They talked fast as they fed the calves that evening, then went to the henhouse to collect eggs, as Naomi and Ruth had a babysitting job at the neighbors'. They were helping out a young Mennonite couple who were celebrating their anniversary in town. Annie and Fannie had wanted to go, but Mam said they were too small.

"Small?" Annie asked Fannie as they returned the calf buckets.

"She meant young," Fannie answered.

"We could have taken care of those children."

"I know. But Mam doesn't."

Annie raced ahead, carrying the wire basket to the henhouse, tripped over the corner of a landscaping tie and fell hard on one knee, producing a nasty cut. She sat in the yard and used the corner of her apron to wipe away the oozing blood, then got to her feet and helped gather the brown eggs from the wooden nests. When one old biddy hen pecked at her, she glared back at her round yellow eyes, reached under, grabbed her waxy legs, and threw her out. She squawked a few times, then sauntered away and pecked at the sawdust.

Fannie went to the hydrant to fill the bucket with fresh water, dumped it into the tin waterer, and moved out the door, only to find the troublesome biddy hen escaping through the opening and down the steps, spreading her wings and squawking as she ran.

"Chase her, Annie!" she yelled.

Annie loved a good chicken chase and took off after her, finally cornering her in the wire fence beside the garden. She flapped and screeched, raced first in one direction, then another, but Annie was the undisputed queen of chicken catching and, with a flying dive, caught one leg as she lunged to the left, Fannie hopping up and down with glee. They laughed the whole way back to the henhouse, their cheeks red with exertion and cold, opened the door, and threw her in without ceremony.

"She should be baked and put into *roascht*."

"She'd be so old and tough, you probably couldn't chop her head off."

"Dat could."

"He probably wouldn't though."

"Maybe for Christmas *roascht*."

"Maybe."

Between them, they swung the wire basket and agreed it had been the best Thanksgiving ever.

Chapter Six

IT WAS RAINING THE MORNING AFTER
Thanksgiving day, a cold, miserable deluge imped-
ing the normal morning chores, with Fannie holding
a large black umbrella while Annie stooped to feed
calves. In spite of Muck boots, coats, and scarves,
they were shivering. The hems of their dresses were
soaked as they ate breakfast.

Mike hitched one of the horses to the buggy and
took them to school, wearing heavy gloves and a
warm coat and beanie. Naomi was allowed to sit on
the front seat with him, of course, since she was oldest, so when Mike looked at her and asked what she
thought of Miriam, they were all a little jealous.

"Pretty cute," Naomi said drily.

"Nice, too, kind and sweet," Mike said, reaching
up to adjust the window latch. Rain pelted against
the buggy, the horse's hooves creating a dull watery
sound, rain splashing from passing vehicles. The
horse was drenched, but he ran on, accustomed to

the heat in summer, cold in winter, rain, wind, just about anything.

"Fancy," Annie offered from the back seat.

"You think?" Mike chuckled.

"Pretty fancy," Fannie repeated.

"Christmas every day?" Annie threw in.

"What? What do you know about that?" Mike asked.

"You said that."

"I guess I did. And, yes, it is like Christmas every day, at least so far. She's a very nice girl."

He was so pleased with himself he needed no response, so no one offered one. Fannie thought Sadie was more attractive, but was polite and respectful of Mike's feelings, so she let it go. She'd read somewhere that love was blind, so perhaps that was the reason he didn't see her imperfections. The skin on her cheeks was not smooth and creamy, but filled with little craters, and she wore glasses, which weren't especially attractive, sort of round and thick. But she had a nice smile and was, in fact, very friendly and kind.

They splashed onto the drive leading to the schoolhouse, and Mike drew aside to let Ben Zook pass on the opposite side, then dropped them off at the porch steps.

"Have a good day," he said cheerfully.

"You too," they called back.

But the day did not prove to be so good. The first thing was learning two new Christmas songs, memorizing the words and the tune, which was seemingly not possible. Teacher Rachel was stressed, which made her voice sort of quivery and off pitch, so that no one was quite sure if she was singing it properly. Becky said she'd heard that song on the radio in a driver's van, and she did not sing the chorus right, then raised her hand and told the teacher what she thought.

Which was not good. Not good at all.

They had their first practice session, which proved disastrous, Teacher Rachel close to tears when Abner refused to speak up or use any form of expression, but stood and read his lines quietly and defiantly. He was the father of a small assembly of pupils, a leading part, but after many attempts, he would not change.

Annie spoke loudly, following everything Teacher Rachel said, eager to get it right. She was playing the part of Alice Mae, the leading gossip at sewing circle, a part meant to make the audience laugh. Annie still felt intimidated by all the lines, but she was eager to impress the teacher. She had already spent time learning the part and didn't want to risk getting switched to another role and having to start over.

The classroom was overheated, the propane gas stove clicking on repeatedly, and the teacher was red-faced and anxious. The lower grades sounded awful as they sang "Away in a Manger," and little Davy was sick all over the floor in singing class, with the sixth grade boys holding their noses and rolling their eyes as Rachel's face became even redder, hurrying over with a roll of paper towels.

No, it was not a good day.

At three o'clock, they all stood on the porch as the rain continued to pelt the approaching teams, the horses standing patiently in line waiting to load their passengers. Sarah was driving, with the window open in order to control the horse better. She spied Teacher Rachel on the porch and waved and called out to her, which produced the first smile of the day for the teacher.

"Quick! Get in, get in. It is pouring. Quick."

"Calm down," Ruth replied.

"Sit in the back. Go. Get in the back." The horse lurched, and Sarah grabbed the reins. "Whoa. Whoa there."

Annie sat in the back and hoped they'd get home safely. Sarah was the worst driver in the county. Excitable, uneasy, she was always slapping her horse or drawing back on the reins, her foot on the brakes, or not watching where she was going, one steel-rimmed wheel sliding off the narrow shoulder of rural roads with a thump, then running along with two wheels in the grass-filled ditch.

"Let me drive," Ruth offered, after they'd jerked back on the road.

"No, you're not fit."

That brought some serious elbows in ribs, with Fannie's ticklish side bringing a surprised squawk, followed by a hilarious round of belly laughs they couldn't stop.

"What's so funny?" Sarah asked, reaching up to wipe the condensation from her side window in order to see the rearview mirror, the two right wheels tipping into the ditch again. "*Ach*, this horse. Seriously."

She jerked the window open, drew hard on the left rein, and almost upset the buggy as it bounced along in the water-filled ditch.

"Stay on the road," Naomi said loudly.

"I'm trying. This horse is so stupid. Come on here. Get out of the ditch."

"It's not the horse. It's the driver," Ruth commented.

No answer.

All the way home, they were either in the ditch or the window was open and Sarah was slapping or yelling or holding back.

The rain continued as they did chores, being careful to watch the adventuresome chicken as they let themselves out. It pounded against the windows of the living room as they huddled side by side with a warm fleece throw to take off the damp chill of doing chores. They studied their lines, repeating the play over and over beneath the soft hissing of the propane gas light, absentmindedly watching the activity of the rest of the family.

In the kitchen, Mam was finishing the dishes, wiping the stovetop with Bar Keepers Friend. Sarah was sweeping the floor, and Becky and Mary were draped across the card table in the corner, working on a thousand-piece jigsaw puzzle. Salome was in one recliner, reading yet another book, with Ephraim and John nowhere to be found. Those boys practically lived outside—or in the barn. They'd said something about building another wren house for Daudy Fisher, but you could never be certain what they were up to. Mam had warned Dat that he'd better crack down on those two, being up to something too much of the time.

Annie and Fannie both thought Dat's eyes twinkled a bit, and they were certain he enjoyed the antics of those two immensely, much more than he'd have Mam know.

Mike and Amos were finishing leftover desserts, talking in quiet tones about being with their girlfriends on Thanksgiving day.

"What did you think, Mam?" Amos asked suddenly.

"About what?"

She rinsed her dishcloth, wrung it out, and hung it carefully on the hook, then turned to face them.

"Our girlfriends."

"They're alright."

The answer was too quick, too clipped to provide approval.

"Come on, Mom."

"Don't call me that. English people say *Mom*. We're Amish."

"Oh, that we are. Are we ever!"

Mam said nothing, crossed her arms, and narrowed her eyes.

"Well, if you want my honest opinion, I think they're both very nice girls, if a bit fancy. Out of the *ordnung* in some ways."

"I knew you'd say that, Mam."

"I don't mean to be critical or harsh, though. It's just that I'm concerned about the next generation. We're losing so many of the old ways. Like, we would never have gone to each other's Thanksgiving dinner, in broad daylight, facing our boyfriend's family. Dating was done secretively."

Mike sighed. "And what was the point? Sneaking around like that."

"We didn't sneak around. It was just done out of respect. It wasn't proper to get too familiar with your boyfriend's family. You stayed away as best you could."

"Why?"

"I don't know why."

"Then why did you do it?"

"I just told you. I guess it was our culture. The way we lived, the way we thought."

"But was it a good thing?"

"I don't know."

"Think about it, Mam. What was good about it?"

"A certain humility. Respect. Shame."

"Why shame? Why was dating shameful? Don't you agree that some change is good? I mean, now you met the girls and you can get to know them, learn to appreciate them. Give us an opinion. As you already have. That's a good thing, right?"

"I guess so."

"Of course it is. Dat and I had a talk, and he's all in favor of becoming acquainted with the girls."

"Dat is a liberal person," Mam said, mincing her words as if her mouth was full of dry meal.

"He's also fair. Thank you for letting them come for dinner. I hope you'll see a lot more of them in the coming months."

When Mam said nothing, they pushed back their chairs and carried dishes to the sink, before Mam said, "I pity Sarah. I guess."

They stood still, watching her.

"I mean, she's getting up in age for a young girl, and I always hoped she'd be asked before you asked a girl. It's different for single girls, who can only wait and pray, not actually be able to change their situation."

"I know." Mike spoke softly, with feeling.

"We'll try and keep it low key for her sake," Amos offered.

"You do that, then. For her."

And Mam whistled low under her breath as she straightened her house, leaned over the card table to check on the jigsaw puzzle's progress, then came to rest with her youngest, Annie and Fannie.

"You can't look at this," Annie said, whisking papers out of reach.

Mam feigned surprise, then covered her eyes with the palms of her hands. "I promise I will not read them, ever."

"You better not."

Above the hiss of the gas light, there was the steady ticking of the clock on the wall, as well as the sluice of rain against the north windows. Bare branches scraped against the glass as the rain and wind blew steadily.

"I would think the waters of the creek would be getting high. I hope Dat doesn't try anything foolhardy."

"Where is he?"

"He has a school board meeting tonight. They're having problems at Locust Run. By the way, have you two been behaving? No more rubber band shooting?"

"Nope. Not us."

"Mam, did you ever consider the fact that we need a riding horse? Just one to share. We don't really want a pony that badly, but rather a real, large, normal horse."

"To ride," Fannie finished for her sister.

"We wouldn't need one for each of us. We could take turns."

Mam nodded. "We'll see what Dat says."

They yawned, stretched, then laid their heads on their mother's shoulders and said sleepily, "Every night we pray for a horse. Not a pony, we say."

Mam smiled, slid an arm around their shoulders, stifled a yawn of her own. She was always aware of neglecting these two, her youngest girls, so independent on their own, having each other as a friend, and often mentoring each other where she should have been.

Twelve children. How had the years brought twelve of them? And none married. It was a blessing but a responsibility. The cares and anxieties, the joys and the sadness. She felt so sorry for Sarah, knowing how much she would enjoy the company of a young man. Somehow, she seemed to have been overlooked

by all the young men in her group, leaving her wondering. She wasn't hideous or gregarious, the way
some girls seemed to repulse young men by being
extremely noisy or desperate. Excitable, a bit dizzy-
ing, but still. Yes, she was happy for Mike and Amos,
but what about Sarah?

And Ephraim brought home western novels from
Jay's Rueben, and Dat had simply shrugged. There
was nothing she could do if he poisoned his mind
with all that shooting and riding and carrying on.
Hard to tell what all they did in those books. And
there was Ben, her own husband, allowing it, leaving
her with no control over the situation. She'd turned
to God in prayer, the way she always did.

"Go to bed, girls," she said, yawning. "Don't forget to say your prayers. Can you say *Unser Vater*?"

Dutifully, they recited the Lord's prayer in perfect
German, in perfect unison, then hugged her tired
shoulders and marched up the stairs. Mam smiled
to herself, thinking how rewarding motherhood was,
despite all the trials. Twins. So uniquely individual,
and yet bound in heart their whole lives.

* * *

Another morning of slogging through the mud with Muck boots and calves with serious cases of scours. Dat had to be told. The rain hit the umbrella. The deluge had not let up all night. Three inches in the rain gauge, nearly four. The sleeping, winding creek ran full, then spread across its banks and became a lake of brown water encroaching on anything in its path. Another wet trip to school and home again, Dat expressing his concern for houses in low-lying areas. The milk truck driver said more days of rain were predicted, and if it rained like this another twenty-four hours, he hoped the bridge over on 432 would hold.

Fannie and Annie's eyes opened wide at the supper table, listening to the boys talk of flooding everywhere. An older gentleman risked his life trying to cross a low part of the road, became stranded when his engine drowned out, and was discovered by a woman walking her French poodle. He was in the hospital being treated for hypothermia.

And still the rain and wind kept up its ceaseless battering. There was no school with the river and its tributaries blocking roads. Some folks were evacuated. The throbbing of helicopter blades was frequent.

But they all felt safe, the farm situated on a hillside, with no chance of being flooded. The roofs were in good repair, the foundation of the house watertight. They thanked God for their good fortune, buying a farm with decent buildings, the strength and sound mind to keep them in good repair.

But Annie and Fannie were restless. They already knew their parts, could recite every line perfectly. They rattled off their lengthy Christmas poem, sang the two new songs, and wished the rain would stop.

They made Triple Treat cookies, beating the shortening and brown sugar with every ounce of strength in their young arms, added eggs and peanut butter, oatmeal, and twice as many chocolate chips as the recipe called for. They overbaked one sheet and underbaked another.

They ran through the rain for the mail, the umbrella waving above their heads like a giant mushroom. Annie spied a rectangular white envelope lying beside the mailbox and quickly bent to pick it up. It was so soggy she couldn't decipher the handwriting, so she tucked it in her coat pocket, then ran to catch up with Fannie who couldn't wait one second, but marched ahead with the umbrella.

She hung up her coat in the laundry room, forgot the soaked letter, and went to find the comics section in the daily paper. On her knees on a kitchen chair, elbows bent over the paper, Fannie came up from behind and gave her a good slap on her bottom.

"Ow!"

"Move over."

Annie did, and Fannie wedged herself into the same chair. Dat came through the door, riffled through the mail, frowned, and asked if this was it.

"Yeah," Fannie answered.

"I'm waiting on a payment for the cows I sent to auction."

Annie pushed out her lower lip, blinked her eyes, and thought of the check. It might be the wet envelope. Quickly she hopped off the chair, retrieved the wet envelope, and handed it to him.

"This it?"

He peered at the blurred handwriting, then drew his head back, raised his eyebrows, gave a long, low whistle. Mam's sewing machine treadle rocked back and forth as she sewed, the firewood popped in the wood stove. Dat held up the envelope, squinted.

"I believe this letter is for Sarah."

Mam's sewing machine rattled on. The clock whirred, chimed twice.

"Malinda?"

Intent on sewing a straight hem, Mam didn't answer. Finally, she stopped, turned her swivel chair. "What?"

"I think this wet letter is for Sarah."

"Well, place it on a dry tea towel. She'll be home at three."

Dat did as he was told. Annie and Fannie continued reading the comics.

"I just don't get it with Garfield. He's not even funny," Annie said, folding the paper neatly and putting it in Dat's magazine holder.

"Funnier than some of the others," Fannie said absentmindedly.

"Mam, what can we do? There's nothing to do."

"Come here. See if this fits."

Annie went first, with Mam placing a black belt apron around her waist, the unhemmed article hanging to the toe of her socks. Mam's arms were soft, her breath warm against her back, a good scent of soap and baking and food coming from her dress front.

"*Ach* my. It's plenty big. You just don't grow."

Fannie had thrown herself against the couch cushions but looked over and said, "That's because she's always running after chickens," then opened her mouth and laughed like a small explosion.

At three o'clock, Sarah came home, threw her sweater across the back of a chair, called out a greeting, and shuffled the mail.

"What's this?" she asked after she'd poured herself a glass of cider.

"What?"

"This. This wet letter on the tea towel. Oh, it's for me."

"Open it then."

Mam's treadle resumed, a dull thwack, thwacking sound.

"Well, it's . . . I don't know if I can open it without ripping this soggy paper."

There was a long silence. So long, in fact, that Annie and Fannie forgot about Sarah standing in the kitchen reading a wet, limp letter on lined tablet paper with very masculine handwriting. They didn't hear her long expulsion of breath or her sinking heavily into a kitchen chair, even as the legs made a scraping sound. They didn't know the cold cider in her glass became lukewarm as she slipped upstairs and forgot about it. And as the treadle of Mam's sewing machine kept up its steady rhythm, light finally broke through rain clouds and fell on the tearful, uplifted face of thanksgiving on her oldest daughter.

Chapter Seven

So now there was Christmas in school, Christmas at home, and the biggest surprise of all was still hidden. Mam pored over catalogs, wrote in her small neat writing, wrote checks, and placed them in various envelopes. She was fully occupied, steadily going down her list of sewing to be done, acquiring gifts through the mail, keeping up with the laundry and cooking and cleaning.

But on Friday afternoon, when Sarah came home from work, the sun shone through the kitchen window, illuminating her face, and with a shock, Mam realized Sarah was glowing. She was literally shining from within.

"Mam?"

The word was lilting, a song in one syllable.

"Why, Sarah, you look positively joyful. Must be you caught the Christmas spirit."

Now she seemed shy, as if it had embarrassed her. Mam was clearly puzzled.

"Uh, Mam. You know that letter? The one on the tea towel?"

"Oh. Yes. I forgot."

"You were busy. The . . . that letter was from Emanuel Beiler." Now she was blushing, her eyes bright with unshed tears.

Mam sat down, her knees suddenly without strength.

"Sarah."

That was all she could manage. It was so unexpected.

"He wants to begin dating. Remember his mother passed away about a year ago? Old Rebecca of the east district?"

"Oh. Oh yes, Sarah. Go on."

"Well, he felt it was his duty to help with her care, and he waited almost five years. Five years, Mam. Can you even imagine what kind of man this is? He has always wanted me. Me!" She crossed her arms on her chest and raised her face to the ceiling. "It's too good to be true."

Mam smiled wisely. "No, Sarah, it's not. You deserve it."

Sarah shook her head. "I don't really, Mam. There were many times I was impatient, grouchy. I tried to tell myself I would accept the lot of being single, but I never did, not really. God must have had a lot of patience with me."

"As He does with all of us," Mam said firmly. She stepped over to Sarah and took her hand in an unusual display of affection. "You have always been my helper, my pillar. An oldest daughter in a family of twelve, and few are the times you have failed me. If ever."

The look between them was a hug without being an actual one.

"See?" Annie said, on the couch wrapped in a warm blanket. "Mam likes Sarah best. She always has."

Fannie shrugged.

When Mam and Sarah made supper together, the kitchen was lit with the joy of their conversation. Mam giggled like a schoolgirl. Sarah laughed out loud, often. At one point they heard Mam say, "Five years, Sarah. My oh. It's just like the great love Isaac had for Rebecca in the Old Testament. My favorite story. *Ach*, Sarah, the Lord is good and faithful."

"I just hope I can be good enough for him. I feel as if he is so much better. A better person. So honorable."

Annie said loudly they were practicing for the Christmas program, but they went right on talking as if she had never opened her mouth.

"Not now, Annie. Mam won't hear us, she's so wrapped up in Sarah."

Annie sighed. She was still cold. She'd slipped on the road and sat in a puddle of water, which left her skirts dripping, the wet, cold fabric slapping against her legs as she walked on home in the wind. She thought Mam didn't seem to have much sympathy for her, saying she shouldn't gawk around the way she did. But that was the difference in being a little girl instead of a big one like Sarah. You just didn't matter as much.

She slid over, closer to Fannie, snuggled up against her, and read a few lines on the page she was reading.

"Are you still cold? I think you're shivering."

"I am. I was wet, and the wind was fierce."

"I know. Poor thing."

They both nodded in unison, and Annie was greatly comforted. If Mam was always occupied with more important matters, the best thing you could have was a twin sister.

* * *

So now, there were three of them dating. It had all happened rather fast. Sarah wasn't actually dating, but she'd say yes, and this all before Christmas. Mam asked Sarah if Emanuel Beiler wouldn't want to come to their Christmas dinner. Sarah looked at her mother quizzically, having seen how she'd responded to her brothers' girlfriends coming for Thanksgiving. Mam sighed and said, well, she might as well move along with the times, since she didn't seem to have much choice in the matter anyway.

There was the Christmas program at school to contend with, and the hope of a horse. Dat was being quiet on the subject, which meant he'd forgotten about it or was keeping a secret. Fannie said if they got anything at all, it would be a pony, probably not even a cart. Annie told her she had to stop saying such depressing things or she was going to sit in the middle of the road and cry.

Teacher Rachel's face was pale and tight at the next play practice. She made Elam Lapp sit in his seat instead of staying behind the curtain like the rest of the class and gave his part to Rueben who was a grade below him. Elam's face was red, and he blinked back tears of shame, but it was his own fault. He never behaved behind the curtain, and this time was the final straw for the teacher. He'd cut a hole in the white curtain, a big one, then went after Emma to cut off her *schtruvels* (wisps of hair).

The program was not going very well. The children were soft spoken, many of them shy. Only two or three of them spoke with the right expression. She gave them a pep talk, then went out on the porch, closed the door, and told them she wanted to be able to hear them recite their poems. There was quite a lot of self-conscious giggling, but most of them stood on the stage, squared their shoulders, opened their mouths, and spoke loudly.

Oh, it was a wonderful time of the year, just like the song. There were brightly colored candy canes with ribbon and holly, colored on both sides and put on the windows with two-sided tape. A manger scene was made out of construction paper and put on the wall between two sets of windows.

Teacher Rachel was an artist, one of the best, and the manger scene would have been much more realistic if she would have done Mary and Joseph herself, but, no, guess who drew them both? Naomi. Who was a major artistic talent in her own eyes, but her classmates weren't so sure.

Annie told Fannie she guaranteed Joseph was not fat, the way Naomi drew him, they had nothing but manna to eat in Bible times. But Fannie corrected her, saying the manna was long gone by the time Jesus was born, and didn't she ever listen to the preacher in church?

Annie was persistent about getting Joseph into better shape, approaching Naomi herself, who agreed, which was almost unbelievable. So she made another one, which proved to be much better.

* * *

There was shopping for gifts, candles in red and green burning in the kitchen, Mam justifying her lack of frugality by saying the red represented the blood of Christ and the green was the grace of God, both of which were the most precious gifts ever given to man.

Dat had a twinkle in his eyes, teased Sarah, telling her he'd stay up on Sunday evening when she and Emanuel came into the kitchen for their coffee, her first date, and her face turned pink and squiggly.

Annie and Fannie beamed with happiness for Sarah. Fannie said the reason Dat had a twinkle in his eye wasn't just Sarah's happiness, it was partly Christmas secrets, stuff he was planning to buy for all his children. But Annie said Mam did the buying, not Dat, and she was very careful of her money, even more than Dat.

"Remember last year?"

"You mean those loops or whatever."

"You know what I mean."

"They made nice potholders."

"How often did we use them?"

"But it was fun making them."

It was true, though, this remembering of Christmases past. Their gifts had been thoughtful, useful items that had not been expensive, but with twelve children to buy for, they were pleased to receive any gift at all. They were a little jealous of some of the gifts their classmates received from their parents, like Barbie dolls with clothes, which their own mother would never consider, saying they were far too worldly. Naomi and Ruth agreed, saying why would they be allowed Barbie dolls if they had never been?

So Annie and Fannie looked forward to small gifts, like coloring books or paint-by-number sets, the kind where you dipped the brush in water, then swirled it in the little circle of paint before you colored in the numbered sections of a picture. They told Mam they would love to have new binder notebooks, the kind containing lots of pockets and hidden zippers to store papers and pens, like the big children had at school, but she only raised her eyebrows and didn't smile, which meant probably not.

Well, it was okay. In spite of everything, Christmas was a happy time, and they could not ruin it by being selfish. Good little girls were appreciative of anything they were given. Plus, Mam told them the *Grischt kindli* (Christ child) was the biggest gift God had ever given, so they must never replace Him with material things.

Whatever she meant by material things. Material was fabric, the cloth she used to sew shirts and trousers and dresses, which weren't Christmas gifts, really. Annie told her sister it would be much easier to appreciate the *Grischt kindli* if you could at least hold Him the way you could hold a tiny newborn, all wrapped up and smelling of baby lotion and soft blankets. Fannie said not all babies smelled good, some of them spit up and smelled like sour milk, plus they scrunched up their faces and cried really loud.

And Dat continued to smile. They often saw his white teeth flashing above his beard, which was really something. The girls asked if he'd go to another horse sale, but he said he didn't believe there was another one before Christmas, shattering their hopes.

They sat in the barn on a bale of straw, listening to the horses munch their hay, discussing the inevitable. They had slim hope of receiving a horse, an even slimmer chance of receiving a horse with a saddle and bridle. If you took the whole family into consideration, how could it be fair to be gifted something costing thousands of dollars?

Annie yanked out a piece of golden straw, put it in her mouth and chewed, before talking around it. "I know, Fannie, but in all seriousness, youngest children are spoiled. We can become spoiled, and it won't really matter."

Fannie's eyebrows shot up. "Yes, it will, Annie. Sarah says we're already *fadarva*. *Gonz schtinkich fadarva.*"

"Spoiled rotten? That's mean. We are not. We don't own half the stuff our classmates do."

"But still. Think about it. We went to the horse sale without bonnets. That's something."

"Plus, we got a box of sixty-four crayons when school started."

They both nodded.

The horses snuffled in their feed boxes, stomped their front feet, and rustled the hay as they reached out for a mouthful. The big workhorses' faces were twice as big as the smaller driving horses, but their eyes were calm and gentle compared to the alert, wild-eyed stare from the more excitable buggy horses. None of them, however, were riding horses. Dat said you could ruin a good driving horse by galloping him, and who wanted to ride a trotting horse? It was hard to do, being jostled up and down with that uneven gait.

But they both loved the horses in spite of not being able to ride. Their coats were sleek and shiny after brushing, the muzzles soft as a baby's skin. You could spend hours brushing manes and tails, leaving them as silky as a head of hair on a person. Or almost. They stood still, quietly allowing Dat to throw a heavy harness on their backs, without flinching, backed into the shafts when he tugged on the britchment and said "Ba-ack."

Fannie couldn't imagine the joy of throwing a saddle across a horse's back, of tightening the girth and slipping the bit into his mouth, sliding the bridle over his sleek ears, then stepping way up onto the stirrup and throwing a leg over like a real cowboy (minus the hat and boots, of course).

Annie visualized the height of being in a saddle, the ground far below, the sky overhead as huge as you could ever imagine. The wind in your face and all that motion with the horse's hooves pounding below you.

Once, at the dentist's office, they watched open-mouthed, unable to tear their gaze from the television set mounted on the wall that was showing real horses with cowboys on their backs, galloping wildly across a dusty prairie. It made them grab the arms of their chairs, chased their heartbeats into a rhythm matching the horse's hooves. They agreed. They could do that. They could ride like the wind if they were ever given a chance.

But now, seated on a bale of straw, it all seemed out of reach. Dat was tight with his money, and every single thing in Mam's view was worldly. Plus, her head was in a pink cloud containing nothing but Mike and Amos and their girlfriends, into which

Sarah came sailing with her chubby little Emanuel Beiler in tow.

They swept the feed aisle, then the forebay, sized up the wall beside the harness cabinet, and said it was the perfect place to hang saddles and bridles.

Supper was steaming hot, a rich, creamy casserole made with noodles and ground beef, a side of spicy baked beans that had roasted slowly in the oven all afternoon. Mam grew huge heads of cabbage in her garden, cut them late in autumn, and stored them in the root cellar, then grated quarters of it and made coleslaw with slivers of bright orange carrot mixed in. There were sweet garlic dill pickles and applesauce, with chocolate cake, vanilla pudding, and canned peaches.

What a wonderful supper, the boys all said, and Mam beamed. She said she enjoyed cooking if she knew it was appreciated, and Dat smiled at her and said, "Always, Malinda. Always."

He loved Mam a whole bunch, you could easily tell, and that made warm, happy circles move around the long kitchen table. Mam wasn't all that lovable, really, the way she was so strict, calling everything worldly. She complained about things not being fixed whenever she thought they should be, like loose drawer pulls and the handle on the commode. She yelled about muddy boots, and her face became fire engine red when Dat spent money on something she disapproved of. She would never say anything about Dat, but she might as well have, the way her head almost exploded with frustration.

On their way to school the following morning, the sky lowered, the air hitting their faces with a damp mist. A few brown oak leaves twirled despairingly on gray branches, the green weeds beside the road appearing trampled by repeated morning frost.

"It's going to snow," Fannie said, swinging her lunch bucket.

"On the first week in December?" Annie asked, catching her lunchbox with her own, resulting in a dull thud.

"Quit it! You'll smash my sandwich."

That warning was largely ignored, except for a cold stare from Ruth, who never did anything wrong herself.

* * *

Practicing for the program was very serious business now. Children labored over rumpled, highlighted copies of poems and plays. Singing was corrected, slowed down or sped up, according to Teacher Rachel's directions. Annie was chosen to start "O Come, All Ye Faithful," which made her nervous the first few times, until she discovered she only had to open her mouth and say "Oh" in a long drawn out way, and the whole class chimed in and sang their hearts out. The sound hit the ceiling, bounced down, and swirled around the room in a joyous rendition of every old Christmas hymn. Her favorite was "God Rest Ye Merry Gentlemen," which Teacher Rachel had sung for them. She looked like an Amish angel, standing up there and singing with confidence, her face lifted to the ceiling, so slim and pretty with her pale blue dress and cape. Annie wished she was beautiful like her.

The reason she liked the new song so much was the fact that they sang it fairly fast, which made it more fun and exciting. "God rest ye merry gentlemen / Let nothing you dismay / Remember Christ our Savior / Was born this Christmas Day." It was a lovely old song, and the children belted it out, putting their hearts into it, mouths open, half smiling, eyes alight. Teacher Rachel praised their ability to sing, and they turned their faces shyly to each other and smiled.

Fannie played the part of "Mother," which Annie thought was not too well thought out, being shorter than her "children." But Teacher Rachel said Fannie had a good voice that carried well, which was very important for this play, so Annie felt proud of her twin sister.

Annie realized Teacher Rachel was very good at doing Christmas plays, the way she praised where praise was due, prodded the slackers, and, if there was open rebellion and refusal to cooperate, eliminated that pupil's part and gave it to someone else. This had appeared unkind to the surly eighth grader, but he had a choice, and he chose to buck the system. Annie heard Ruth tell Naomi she pitied Elam, but Naomi disagreed, saying he'd had two weeks to speak up and do it right. Ruth obviously had a crush on Elan, the way she laughed too loud and her face turned pink when he was around, but no one was ever allowed to mention that kind of thing in school.

They made paper chains out of red and green construction paper and hung them from the four corners of the classroom to a point in the middle, then created a large, golden star representing the star that guided the wise men to the stable to worship the Baby Jesus. It must have been a cold night, the way those wise men were bundled up with all those robes, crazy hats, and scarves they wore. Annie wondered why they were called wise men, and Fannie shrugged her shoulders and said how would she know, she wasn't alive in Bible times. Naomi said they were men that searched the Scriptures and knew the Messiah would be born around this time.

"Boy, that *is* wise, isn't it?" she answered, and received a nice, wide smile from her, which was really something.

* * *

Saturday night arrived, which meant Sarah had a boyfriend, officially now. The twins caught a glimpse of him when he climbed out of his buggy and stood beside his horse, waiting for Sarah, who was about the same height. But wearing that heavy black coat, they couldn't tell if he was, in fact, overweight, but his hair shone like a copper penny in the sunlight.

"Short and red-haired," Annie said quietly.

"Sarah isn't much to look at. Not like Teacher Rachel," Fannie said.

"So you think they're a good couple?"

"Of course. Boys don't ask a girl on account of their looks."

Annie thought Fannie ended her sentence with a sniff, the kind of sniff that meant she knew a lot more than Annie, which set her into argument mode immediately. They had a healthy discussion about this, which Mam overheard from the kitchen and nipped effectively in the bud by saying they were far too immature to be having this discussion, and it was high time they went to bed, so they brushed their teeth and gathered up their books and obeyed.

Lying side by side, Annie brought up the subject again.

"I guarantee you, Fannie, a really tall handsome boy is not going to look twice at a homely, fat girl."

"You don't know. You have no idea. Mam says if a man asks God for a wife, He'll direct him to the one He has for him."

"Mam doesn't tell you that kind of thing."

"I overheard her tell Sarah."

Then, because she was a little bit peeved, Annie turned her back and went to sleep. So did Fannie. But during the night, when they felt cold, they snuggled together and had forgotten their tiff by morning.

Chapter Eight

CHRISTMAS WAS IN THE AIR AND EVERY-
where they looked. Sarah sat at the kitchen table with
Mam and discussed a proposed shopping trip now
that she had a boyfriend to buy for. Mike and Amos
had no clue what to get their girlfriends either. There
weren't many stores in there area, so they all planned
a trip to Owensboro, which was quite a big city, one
they had only been to once or twice. Naomi begged
to go. Mary, Becky, and Salome were allowed, but
not Naomi and Ruth and certainly not the twins.
This trip was out of necessity, not for pleasure, Mam
said firmly, but she had two bright spots on her
cheeks and her eyes were sparkling, so they knew it
wasn't strictly necessity.

All they could do, in the end, was sit glumly
and watch everyone get ready, rushing around
getting dressed, gathering purses and brushing
coats. Excitement ran high. They hummed catchy
Christmas tunes like "Up on the Housetop" about

Santa Claus, which was childish, the way no one believed in the made-up version of Christmas. But it was a celebration, this season, with three of her children past the age of being chosen, getting married, probably, finally, and Mam would certainly do her part in making it happen.

When the twelve-passenger van pulled in, they all rushed out the door, telling the four girls to be *brauf*. A feeling of being marooned, a certain kind of desolation settled over all four of them, until Fannie said the chickens hadn't been tended, and Annie got her coat, dragged her scarf over her head, and tied it hard under her chin. She wasn't necessarily in a good mood and told Fannie so.

"Nothing we're going to do to change it. We're expected to obey."

"I know. But I'm mad. If these chickens are out of their pen, I'm going to *kepp* them."

Fannie howled and laughed, bent over double. "How will you do that?"

"With an axe," she said smartly, trying to keep a straight face.

Sure enough, two chickens dashed out between their legs, both red hens, those unruly Rhode Island Reds. With a thin layer of snow and ice on the grass, the chickens had good enough traction, their sharp claws digging straight through the slippery crust, but not Annie's Muck boots. She took off after them, slipped and fell flat on her stomach, her face smashed into the cold, hard crust, her bare knees hitting it as well. She had a nasty cut on her eyebrow and a brushburn on her knee, but paid her injuries no heed. She scrambled to her feet and took off again, Fannie laughing uproariously.

It wasn't all that funny, for sure, so she bent to the task, her boots making loud crashing noises as they hit the thin layer of crackly ice and snow. Chickens shouldn't be out in the snow like this, she reasoned to herself, her breath coming in hard little puffs. She finally gave up, went back to the chicken house for the long wire hook, and renewed her efforts, snaking the hook efficiently to grab one waxy, yellow leg to yank the bird off its feet and back into the chicken house.

The small area was always a bit dusty, cloudy, and acrid with the smell of their droppings. But the nests were clean with new shavings, the white and brown eggs clean and warm, the hens pacing around with their round yellow eyes watching warily.

Chickens were like that. You could never be certain they were friendly. You could never hold a chicken and stroke its feathers the way you could hold a cat or a small dog. Chickens weren't to be trusted, the way they could lash out and peck your hand with their sharp beaks, hard enough to draw blood.

Fannie carried the basket of eggs, gingerly placing one foot in front of the other. These eggs were necessary, breakfast for the whole family, all fourteen of them. They set the wire basket on the counter in the laundry room and divested themselves of coats and scarves before placing the eggs in cardboard boxes. The kitchen had a warm cozy atmosphere after the damp chill outside, with Naomi and Ruth at the table, a pile of cookbooks strewn everywhere.

"I never made caramel popcorn in my life," they heard Ruth say.

"Come on, Ruth. We'll never know if we don't try."

"I'm not cooking that caramel stuff. You don't know how, either."

"The instructions are very simple."

"This could be interesting," Annie whispered to Fannie.

"First, the popcorn. Easy," Ruth said.

"I'll cook the caramel. Do we have peanuts?"

Annie and Fannie settled in for the show, anticipating an extremely interesting disaster. Naomi was skilled at believing herself far above her own capabilities, taking on tasks proving to be her undoing. Not too long ago, she tried to make shoofly whoopie pies, which she loved, resulting in absolute failure, the normally soft molasses cookie with brown sugar frosting turning out to be inedible, even dipped in milk. And here she was, taking on caramel popcorn.

The sauce bubbled. Naomi stirred. And stirred some more.

Ruth peered over her shoulder at the saucepan. "Surely it cooked long enough," she said.

Annie and Fannie shared a long, meaningful look.

"Five minutes."

The kitchen was quiet, except for the ticking of the clock and the slow bubbling from the saucepan. Then the bubbling changed to a *blup-blup* kind of sound. Naomi stirred furiously, her face red.

"Take it off," Ruth shrieked suddenly. "Naomi, get it off the burner."

"But I have to add a cup of milk."

"Do it quickly then."

All Annie and Fannie could remember was the cold milk hitting the boiling caramel, a loud hiss, and a cloud of steam, a wooden spoon thrown at the countertop, and Naomi clawing at her cheekbone, followed by an ear-splitting shriek.

"Ow! Ow!"

"Cold water. Quick, Naomi."

Hunched over, Naomi scuttled to the sink, emitting shrieks coupled with long drawn-out wails, before sloshing cold water on her face like a person dying of thirst. Ruth stood beside her, asking intermittently if she was alright, or should she get Dat?

The saucepan was left to boil, blupping away on the blue-ring gas flame, as everyone's attention turned to Naomi's injury. When they finally remembered the cooking caramel, it was way beyond salvaging, so they set it off the burner and watched as Ruth brought the B & W salve, the miracle for burns.

"The heat has to come out first," Naomi wailed, real tears coursing down her cheeks along with the cold water.

It was pitiful, really, watching Naomi in so much pain. Annie felt sorry for every moment she'd been mad at her. She was quite bossy, really, but when someone was in pain, you always wished them well.

Ruth applied the B & W very gently, which soothed the burning sensation very quickly. Naomi was lying on the couch with her arm across her forehead, being quiet and brave, really, so Annie made scrambled eggs with American cheese and salt and pepper for her and a glass of chocolate milk with plenty of Hershey's syrup.

When Dat came home with Ephraim and John, she made some for them too, and they made egg sandwiches with deer bologna and mayonnaise.

"Where were you?" Fannie asked, after Dat had checked Naomi's burn, which wasn't all that bad for the fuss she'd made.

"Oh, out and about. Getting Roger shod. He threw a shoe on the way to church."

The expression "threw a shoe" always brought to mind a horse rearing back on his hind legs and throwing a shoe with his front ones, instead of the way it really happened, the iron horse shoe loosening and flying off to rest on the road somewhere.

"What else did you do?"

Ephraim and John acted strangely, the way they rolled their eyes in one direction, then tried not to smile. But only Annie noticed this, and when she told Fannie, she made a sound like air coming out of a tire with a hole in it, saying her imagination was out of control.

"Well, Fannie, I don't care what you say. If they took Roger to be shod, they could have talked to Henry Beiler about a horse for us. He shoes lots of horses, so Dat could easily have explained about a horse for Christmas. For us, for me and you."

"Which he very likely didn't do."

"I know." Suddenly she brightened. "But he could have."

* * *

When Mam and the older siblings returned, the spirit of Christmas was so thick you could taste it on your tongue. Plastic bags were whisked into the bedroom closet, long rolls of gift wrap stuck out of other shopping bags like thick antennae. There was scotch tape and fancy ribbon, books, pictures to hang on the wall, astonishing things they could never imagine their mother buying. But she had approved of the boys buying the beautiful, heavy framed prints at a Christian bookstore, for a price which would be kept secret for decades.

And Sarah had not been timid either, purchasing a large, glossy book of western scenery and stories of settlers in a foreign land, a long, rectangular box of fine chocolates, and a shirt with a tiny, bumpy design in the fabric. Her face was flushed with pure happiness, her eyes shining so that she seemed almost beautiful.

That evening they brought in a DeWalt battery lamp and hung it on a hook above the table, pushed the propane lamp to the side, and proceeded to wrap these fine, quality gifts.

It was a grand moment for the whole family, a new and exciting adventure, wrapping these things for actual girlfriends and Sarah's boyfriend, too, which made it doubly wonderful. Mam hovered and fluttered about like an excited bird, and Dat sat back, drank his tea, and smiled with his teeth showing again.

Annie said Dat's teeth weren't showing only on account of the gifts they'd bought, it was another secret as well, that she'd caught Ephraim and John passing some sort of look between them. She pestered Mam, asking what was in the bedroom closet, and she said it was the boys' Christmas gifts but not for her to know about.

They ate some of the chocolate-covered peanuts Mam had bought for them, but felt a bit left out, as if they were of no importance at all. Which they weren't, they supposed, and drifted away to eat the popcorn that had never received its caramel sauce.

These days, many things went unnoticed, even Naomi's burn, until she showed it to Mam, who clucked a bit absentmindedly, but didn't pity Naomi much, saying she shouldn't have attempted something that complicated, and Sarah, what did you do with the ribbon you bought?

Naomi hid the saucepan with the caramel now cooled, as hard as a rock. She had no idea how the saucepan would ever be used again, but it turned out to be Mam's favorite, and war was declared until it was found. Once the pan was produced Mam merely filled the teakettle, boiled water, and poured it in before removing the melting caramel.

Sarah's gifts were wrapped in very pretty black and gold wrapping paper with a black ribbon holding all of the boxes together in a heap. With a red and gold assortment of ribbons on top, it was breathtaking, and Sarah was so pleased and excited, it was a true Christmas joy.

"Oh, she deserves it, if anyone ever did," Mam said.

"She surely does," Dat nodded.

The load of being the oldest child of twelve had fallen on Sarah's young shoulders at a stage in life when many girls were still carefree. When babies were born, she learned to do laundry, scrub floors, and wash dishes, rock toddlers to sleep, and cook simple meals, always aware of jobs piling up for Mam, who wasn't sleeping well with the new baby, her strength depleted in childbirth. Maybe that was why her shoulders were rounded, her figure a bit bent, with an air of maturity surpassing most girls her age. And why she found it hard to be silly and frivolous at times.

And then, quite unexpectedly, Emanuel Beiler himself stood in the kitchen, his heavy black coat opened in front, a blue shirt underneath. Sarah seemed calm as she watched him shake hands with Dat, then Mam. Ephraim and John solemnly extended a hand, then went back to their books, peeping over the top occasionally. When he greeted Annie and Fannie, he stepped back and said he doubted whether he would ever be able to tell them apart. They were pleased, finally having a bit of the spotlight for themselves, and decided immediately they liked Emanuel Beiler, short, red-haired, and pink-faced or not. He was super nice. Nicer than Dat or Mike or Amos.

He asked how old they were, and if they would like to go see the Christmas tree at the Church of God next Saturday night. Ruth and Naomi too. Sarah was so proud, so pleased, one hand holding the other across her waist, looking a bit matronly.

They heard Dat tell Mam she'd be "making a wedding" next year. *Hochtzich mocha.* Mam shook her head in denial, giggled and sputtered like a schoolgirl, her hand held across her mouth as she kept smiling. She slapped Dat across his forearm playfully, and he caught her hand and smiled so nicely at her.

Oh, Christmas was simply everywhere. It reverberated from the closet in the bedroom, shone in black, red, and gold from Sarah's room, whispered from Mike and Amos's room where the beautifully wrapped pictures in their cardboard were stacked against the wall.

Annie had another grand idea. If the boys' gifts were in the bedroom closet, then they had no gift at all. Not one, which meant Dat's teeth said he was buying a horse for them. Or had already bought it. Fannie said she'd better learn to give up, but her eyes gleamed in a happy sort of way, and Annie knew she might agree that Dat was up to something.

Mam began her Christmas cookie baking, which meant she'd be baking for days and days. She made her mother's traditional recipes and tried new ones every year. When the girls got home from school in the afternoon, an array of cookies waited to be packed away in containers and taken to the freezer. She made sugar cookies with drizzled white chocolate, molasses cookies dipped in white chocolate, and chocolate cookies with half of a marshmallow pressed into them, then placed back in the oven till the marshmallows were puffy, taken out and cooled, then frosted with chocolate buttercream frosting. She made raspberry jam strips, date balls, pecan tarts, coconut macaroons, and lemon bars. The boys ate many of them, but mostly they were safely ferried to the freezer for platters for the neighbors and for the family to enjoy for the holidays.

Then, when Annie was almost positive they were actually receiving a horse for Christmas, two cardboard boxes arrived by UPS, covered in wrapping paper with Christmas trees and deer all over it, and name tags with "Annie" written on one, "Fannie" on the other, then set on the drop leaf table in the living room with everyone else's wrapped gifts.

Their disappointment was large and very heavy, as if the cardboard boxes were placed directly on their chests. A gift of their own, especially one that size, meant that was all they were getting, and all thoughts of a horse must be banished. They hid their true feelings, even from each other, put books to their faces, and wiped an occasional tear that escaped from their resolve.

Finally, when they lay side by side in the semi-darkness, a cold moon sailing across the sky in the battering winter wind, Fannie whispered Annie's name, and she didn't answer, the lump in her throat obstructing words.

"Annie," she said out loud.

"I should have stopped you from saying those things."

"You mean about a horse?"

"Yes"

"You tried."

There was a bit of silence as tree branches raked across the vinyl siding. A loose shutter flapped a bit before settling down.

"We'll be alright without a horse."

"Yes. Mam says everyone has to give up their own will."

"What do you think would be big enough to put in that package?"

"Probably a skateboard. Or a Kan Jam game. Maybe volleyball."

"All of them would be great."

"It's sad, though. It's sad if parents have no clue how badly their children want a horse."

"Mmhmm."

Then, as if all of this wasn't bad enough, Teacher Rachel caught the twins whispering to Susan, and they were stuck inside for recess, again, writing one hundred sentences about school rules. Why Susan was let go was hard to understand, but they said nothing, till they walked home, swinging their lunchboxes and scuffing at gravel.

Naomi said Susan wasn't whispering, that was why. Ruth said she couldn't help it, it wouldn't have been fair to punish her, and besides, they knew better. No whispering was the rule.

When no one was looking, Annie made a face at Ruth and Naomi's backs, which made her feel a lot better. Fannie kicked gravel most of the way home, which Annie thought wouldn't help at all.

One thing, though, the Christmas program was going really well finally. They were set to have one of the best plays ever, the best singing and hardly any long, boring poems spoken in an unintelligible monotone. And two more days, and they'd go with Emanuel and Sarah to see the Christmas tree, which wasn't a real one, but a stage in an auditorium made up of dozens of men and women in the choir, shaped like a Christmas tree, all singing hymns to accompanying organ music.

Annie decided on her own to give it another shot and stood behind a cow where Dat was crouched, holding on to the milking machine the way he sometimes did. He looked up at her, smiled, and squinted his eyes.

"Now what?" he asked, teasing

"Well, I was hoping for a horse for Christmas, but there are two pretty big boxes wrapped for me and Fannie, so I guess you couldn't put a horse in them, right?"

"I'm afraid not."

"Are horses terribly expensive?"

"Yes, they really are."

"Okay then. So we're not getting one, me and Fannie, right?"

"Well, I would truly consider it, Annie, knowing how badly you would like to own one, but milk prices are low, and it wouldn't really be fair to spend that much on the two of you without spending a lot on the rest of the family."

"Right."

Her shoulders slumped, even as she agreed. She took a deep breath, lifted her shoulders for courage, and walked steadily out of the cow stable. Some people like Fannie could give up in one big gulp, swallow the whole cupful of disappointment at once, and some people had to take it one teaspoon at a time.

She had one more trick up her sleeve that was worth a try, but it would carry more weight if Fannie would help.

As she fed calves, she thought of "giving up" as something that made no sense, and how it just didn't seem right. How could they think like this, when the minister in church said God gave His children all manner of gifts, and who would give their son a stone if he asked for a fish? She didn't want a fish. Only a horse.

And then the thought hit her. What if it was a glass aquarium in that box? And Mam was secretly feeding fish? She told her older sisters about this horrible thought, and all three of them laughed so hard they almost choked, so she threw a whole handful of gravel at them, which only made them laugh harder.

The Christmas spirit had evaporated for Annie.

Chapter Nine

IN THE BACK SEAT OF EMANUEL'S BUGGY, THE four girls were packed like sardines in a tin, but no one was complaining. This was one of the best things ever, listening to them, secretly learning how to talk to your boyfriend when the time came. Emanuel was quite talkative, his voice a bit high for a young man, but he was always polite and kind in his observations. He turned around to ask if they weren't packed in there too tightly, which they were, but said no, no, it was fine.

They met Mike and Amos and their fancy girlfriends with their skirts almost to the tips of their shoes. Miriam was even wearing a coat with a hood on it, which would be absolutely *schrecklich* (terrible) for Mam to see. A large group of people were going through the doors of the church, and lots of English people had hoods on their jackets, so it must be in style.

Emanuel put his hand on Sarah's elbow to guide her along, which Annie thought was so nice of him. They were all seated on folding chairs in the huge, high vaulted ceiling area, and the stack of people dressed in green was amazing. It really was like a live Christmas tree. And when they began to sing, it was like being caught up in a wave of sound, carried up and up with the accompanying organ music until she thought surely she must be with the angels above the stable. She saw Emanuel wipe a tear, then Sarah.

It was a wonderful night. At the door, Emanuel asked if they'd like to walk across the road and down about a hundred yards to Burger King for a sandwich. The girls had never been there, but they didn't say that, just walked along under the yellow glow of streetlights and through the glass doors of the fast food place, where the white lights were almost blinding. Luckily, Sarah sat them at a round table, said she'd order for them, and they slid back and forth on the slippery bench, giggled, and had a great time until Emanuel brought their food.

It was all delicious, especially the French fries dipped in little cups of ketchup. Emanuel had a huge sandwich called a Whopper, and so did Sarah, but the girls had chicken nuggets, which were delicious. Naomi and Ruth even flirted a bit with Emanuel, thinking they were real *rumschpringa*, which they weren't, but it was no big deal. They talked and laughed together easily. Emanuel was so nice to be with, so easy to say anything and not feel stupid or judged for your behavior.

They hurried back to the buggy, where the blanketed horse stood patiently waiting in the cold, hopped in the back, and were glad for the warmth. They sang Christmas songs on the way home, and Emanuel pretended to pound organ keys, going "Dah-da!" real loud at the end of the song.

Oh, he was so nice. Certainly, Sarah would be blessed.

Mam beamed at them from her recliner, all wrapped up in her warm housecoat with the scent of talcum powder and deodorant, her hair washed and put in a ponytail. Annie sat on one arm of her chair, Fannie on the other, and they told her every detail, including the French fries and ketchup. Sarah stayed outside a while, talking to Emanuel.

"Did you thank him for your supper?" she asked.

"Yes, yes, we did, Mam."

"We all remembered."

"You're good girls, all four of you. Well, I'm glad you had a good time, but it's off to bed now. We have a busy day tomorrow, helping clean Daudy and Mommy's house for Christmas."

Annie and Fannie couldn't go to sleep with the bright moonlight streaming through the window, the excitement of the evening lingering as they talked. Wasn't Miriam fancy, though? Oh, she looked terribly nice. They'd have a hard time getting away with dressing like that, though, with Mam being so strict. They decided Emanuel was the nicest young man they ever met, absolutely.

They were back in another buggy the following morning, the four of them again, with Mam driving the seven miles to Daudy's house. Sarah and Salome were doing the laundry and weekly cleaning at home, so Mam felt free to pay her parents a visit and to help get their house spruced up for Christmas.

Annie chattered in the front seat, wanting to impress Mam, as grownup as she felt, with her sisters in the back. They took turns, kept careful tabs on whose turn it was to sit with Mam, so everything would turn out to be fair.

"Can I drive, Mam?"

"*May* I?"

"May I drive?"

She handed the reins over, and Annie scooted toward her mother as closely as she could, so it would feel as if she was the real driver. The window was closed, with the reins through a small rectangular hole in the frame, so she couldn't really experience the feel of the horse's mouth the way she could when the window was open. When you drove a horse with the window open, the horse's mouth tugged on the reins a bit, and you felt a wonderfully cool sensation, as if you were driving a stagecoach or Cinderella's carriage made from a pumpkin, although Annie never told anyone that thought, knowing they'd think she was going way overboard.

Which she was, perhaps, but what was wrong with that? Just because you were an Amish girl in a plain gray and black buggy going slowly down the road didn't mean you couldn't imagine other, more exciting ways of travel.

Clunk.

"Watch it there. Mam, are you letting Annie drive?"

"Draw on the left rein, Annie," Mam said patiently.

A lurch, and the buggy settled back on the macadam road. There was a collective groan from the back seat.

"You drive, Mam," from bossy Naomi.

"Oh, let her go for a while yet."

That was the trouble with being the youngest. Everywhere you went, you were bossed around by older siblings.

Annie sat up straight, squared her shoulders, and concentrated on keeping the horse in perfect line, not too far away from the shoulder but avoiding the yellow line. Mam hummed low beneath her breath, and the girls chattered among themselves as the steel-rimmed tires ground against the macadam, the steady rhythm of the horse's hooves drumming on.

Mommy Fisher was always so glad to see them, opening the door the minute she caught sight of an approaching team, throwing it wide as she welcomed them in.

"Someone should have been here to help you with the horse," she said first, always concerned about others' welfare.

"Oh, no, Mam, not at all. Daudy has a clean stable."

Their grandfather was known as *Daudy*, the Pennsylvania Dutch word for grandfathers. He was Mam's father, stooped and elderly, his balding head circled by wispy white hair, his beard long and white as well. He peered through small round glasses, perched on a nose of tremendous size, with blue and purple veins crisscrossing like roads on a map. He smiled widely, his old dentures tipping a bit, that ever-present danger presenting itself once again.

Annie and Fannie had an open discussion about Daudy's dentures, and both agreed he should see a dentist or wherever you went to do something about loose teeth. Once, Annie had made him laugh out loud, and his dentures went flying out of his mouth.

Oh, it was a sight, Daudy with no teeth. His whole face fell in, his nose seeming even larger.

"Malinda. And here are the girls."

He shook hands warmly, his old hands thick and dry. Amish grandparents rarely hugged their grandchildren, but instead took their hands and shook a bit.

"So nice of you, Malinda. I know you have plenty to do."

"I always do. You know that."

They looked at each other with an understanding. Mommy had raised a family of fourteen children, and she well knew the workload, about how you had to make time for yourself—and one of Mam's earthly pleasures was hitching up faithful Sue and driving to her elderly parents.

Mommy was round as a barrel and a bit taller than Daudy, her eyes dark and quick as a bird, although she walked with a limp on account of her right knee.

"Now, you're sitting down for a *schtick*."

A *schtick* was the Dutch word for piece, a small piece of a meal, like a snack. Mam had called ahead and left a message letting them know they'd be coming, so Mommy had been delighted to prepare more than a few treats.

The coffee was piping hot, the hot chocolate on the back of the stove. The small kitchen was bright and sunny, the teakettle humming on the polished range top, the linoleum gleaming. There was a vinyl tablecloth with a blue-checkered design, a lazy Susan in the middle with a sugar bowl, salt and pepper shakers, a plastic honey bear about half full of honey, napkins, and at least fifteen pill bottles. Mam's coffee mug said #1 GRANDPA.

There were chewy chocolate chip cookies and sticky buns with caramel icing and little cups of fruit. There were slices of French toast with syrup and a breakfast casserole made with cheese, bacon, onion, and peppers, and real toast Mommy fired in a pan with butter.

Annie and Fannie dipped chocolate chip cookies in their hot chocolate, which never crumbled and went to nothing the way Oreos did. You could dip these cookies for a long time and they stayed intact. The breakfast casserole wasn't very good, not with onion and green peppers in it, so Annie fed some of hers to Cindy, the little Yorkshire terrier that owned Mommy's house.

Cindy was terribly spoiled. She had never been housebroken, but peed on the rug inside the door, which Mam thought was disgusting, but never said a word to Mommy.

Oh, how they talked. Daudy didn't say very much, but he chuckled a lot, and sometimes shook his head. Mam went on and on about Emanuel Beiler and Sarah, which made Mommy weep a little bit. Mam said Miriam, Mike's girlfriend, was "out of the *ordnung*," which concerned her, but Mommy said Mam had to be careful, not everyone was raised the same. Sometimes you had to move with the times, not be so stuck in your ways that it made life hard for those around you.

Mam drank her coffee and didn't say much for a while.

Ruth and Naomi were sent outside to rake leaves out of the flower beds and dump them on the garden. The air was still and very cold, so they muttered quietly to themselves about the chore. Annie and Fannie were gleeful, being allowed to stay inside and wash dishes. Daudy put on his overcoat and straw hat, pulled on a pair of work gloves, and went out to help.

Daudy and Mommy lived on the same farm they'd bought in the eighties, when they moved to Kentucky. After Daudy became too old to run the farm, his oldest son Jonas took over. They built a small *Daudy haus* (home for older parents) on the same property, a few feet from the main farmhouse, with a small yard and garden of their own.

Lizzie, Jonas's wife, was a bighearted woman who never harbored a thought for herself, but was always caring about her aging in-laws. Mommy said they couldn't have it any better, but Daudy sometimes complained about Jonas spending money for a better milking system, a new bulk tank, replacing things Daudy thought were just fine.

Mommy's pantry smelled weird. You'd think a grandmother's pantry would smell like sugar and candy, good things like chocolate and cinnamon. It was a strong smell of something like vinegar or rotting cheese or black licorice. Mam said Mommy and Daudy didn't eat their potatoes fast enough, and some of them went bad in the wooden bin.

Nothing smelled worse than rotting potatoes.

After the dishes were washed and dried, they were sent to wash the windows in the barn. Daudy loved barn swallows, which built nests in the rafters, so the barn was really messy. But it was warm and dry, so they had nothing to complain about. Annie stood in the middle of the forebay and imagined out loud, saying what if this was their barn, and they each had a riding horse, a brown Morgan or a black quarter horse?

"If I ever have a horse, I will braid his mane and put pink ribbons in it. And his tail. Plus, I'd have stuff to spray on his coat to make it shiny, and he'd run with his neck arched," Annie said.

Fannie said nothing as she sprayed Windex on the dusty window splattered with bird droppings.

"And if there are pink ribbons in his mane, I'd have a pink saddle blanket to match. And, if I was English, I'd wear a white cowboy hat with a pink ribbon."

Fannie turned to look at her sternly. "Annie, that's *hochmut* (haughty), and you know it. Stop talking like that."

"Sometimes you act just like Mam, Fannie. I said *if* I was English."

"Well, you're not."

"I know that."

"Then stop talking like that." She squirted more Windex, wiped round and round, creating a pattern of white streaks. "Why would Daudy allow all these birds in his barn?" Fannie asked, setting down the roll of paper towels.

"They eat flies. And they're cute."

"They are cute. But I'd rather have flies. They don't splatter up a barn nearly as bad as this."

The door opened and Daudy stuck his face through the opening.

"How's it going in here?"

"Oh, pretty good," Annie said quickly.

She didn't really want him to come in because he was so hard of hearing. He said "What?" so often you finally yelled out the words slowly and then he told you that you didn't need to yell. Besides, there was the danger of falling dentures, which was not something they needed to experience again.

He went back out and closed the door.

"Good. He's helping Ruth with the garden cart."

As they worked, they dreamed of horses, all kinds of horses. They thought of the rescued animals from the kill pen. You could go visit them and pick out a horse the way you could get a dog at the shelter for small animals. The horses were inexpensive.

"Yes, Fannie, but they're probably broken-down, old pitiful creatures that can't even gallop. With ribs and coarse hair and a big belly and broken hooves. I want a nice horse, a big, strong, shiny one, with a thick mane and tail."

Fannie nodded.

"I understand. But they all come with a big price tag."

"I know."

It was fun to daydream, to plan and discuss a horse, even if you could never have one.

After the windows were finished, they were allowed to help Mommy wrap her small Christmas gifts. She always bought something for everyone, all forty-four of her grandchildren, even if it was only a Berenstain Bears book or a little plastic packet of combs. Sometimes the boys received a white mug with their name on it to put on their dresser, or a small pocket knife for the older ones.

Every gift was wrapped in cheap, colorful wrap from the dollar store, and there was never any ribbon. But it was exciting, watching Mommy line up all her items and putting them in groups, fussing and talking about how much she enjoyed giving gifts to her grandchildren, and how precious were the small keepsakes she'd received from her own grandmother, way back when there weren't very many Amish people.

"Why are there more now?" Annie asked.

"Oh, well, people marry and have children," Mommy clucked.

That was a good answer. Like Sarah and Emanuel. Or Mike and Miriam and Amos and Sadie.

It felt so wonderful, knowing her oldest siblings were actually chosen by someone to be their companion for their whole life. That was a long time. It must take a lot of thought to decide to go ahead and get married.

Mommy laughed and laughed when Annie told her about this.

"Yes, Annie, that's the way it is. Daudy and I have been together fifty-four years."

"Do you still like him?" Annie asked, thinking of his nose and those slippery dentures.

"Why, of course. Why wouldn't I?" she chortled.

"Here, Fannie, wrap this for Isaac. He's about at the age where he won't want a toy."

Fannie held up the small plate with a picture of a bluebird on it, thought of burly, big-mouthed Isaac, his too-tight trousers with the pockets straining at the buttons, and held up the delicate porcelain plate. She raised her eyebrows at Annie, and they both had to look away very quickly.

"He's such a nice boy. I think he'll appreciate that plate. He can keep it on his desk or dresser and put his little treasures on it. You know how boys collect rocks and feathers and nails, stuff like that."

Annie remembered last Christmas, when he teased her without mercy, imitating the way she'd said her poem at the program. He'd squared his shoulders and set his voice to a high squeak, copying every word. She'd felt a lump rise in her throat and walked away, but Fannie let him have it. She wasn't going to stand there and let him make fun of her twin sister. She told him he needed to apologize. Which he never did of course, but still.

So, the bluebird plate was the perfect gift for Isaac.

They left the house spotless, floors shining, windows gleaming in the cold sunshine, the bathroom smelling of Mommy's Lysol cleaner and a fresh towel rinsed in Downy on the towel rack. The porch was swept, the rug shaken and replaced, the geraniums on the south side pinched back and watered inside in the enclosed porch.

Mommy was so grateful, there were tears in her eyes, and Daudy said they'd never forget their kindness, even if they lived to be a hundred, and Mam laughed, told him he was almost there.

Sometimes when Mam was with her parents, she seemed younger, more talkative, even sort of *groossfiehlich* (proud), talking the way young girls did. Annie thought it was only to make Mommy chuckle and shake her head, but Fannie said it was probably the way she used to be before she had all those children, and when she was with her parents, she felt young again. Whatever it was, they loved going to Daudy's house, loved the good feeling of having done something worthwhile, carrying Mommy's thanks like a sweet scent in the buggy.

Sue trotted fast, knew she was going home, so that when Mam spied a sign at the local produce place, she could barely stop fast enough to make the turn.

Citrus fruit by the case. Yes, indeed. Flu season was coming on, and she'd need cases of navel oranges, grapefruit, tangerines. "My oh," she said. "My oh. What a good price. Can hardly believe they come from Florida already."

She bought four cases of each.

"We have a big family," she informed the jovial man at the register. "These oranges won't last long."

"You folks generally do," he nodded, eyeing Mam with a mixture of awe and patience. "Don't know how you women do it."

She smiled demurely, then lifted the lid of the buggy door in the back and stacked all the boxes where the seat had been. It was set on top, leaving no room for the girls, so they all crowded in front, in layers: Mam, Naomi, and Ruth on the bottom, Annie and Fannie on them, leaving only enough room for Mam and the reins. Sue trotted at a fast pace, uphill and down, until dark sweat stains appeared below her harness and her breath came in short puffs. But horses could run for miles if allowed to run at their own pace, even if they sweated. And Sue was happy to be going home to her stable, drawing the buggy and all its contents.

Chapter Ten

THE BIG DAY FINALLY ARRIVED, THE EVENING of the long-awaited Christmas program. The children had worked and worked, the teacher agonizing over details. The blackboard had become a wondrous thing. Colored chalk was the best invention ever, the way Teacher Rachel created a manger scene with a large, hovering angel in attendance. She'd worked on it every evening for a week, and every day the children were amazed at what she'd done. She was an artist, and it certainly showed. She did apologize for not allowing the children to help, but it was her own project, just for the holidays.

It wasn't really the whole manger scene, just the manger with a swaddled baby Jesus and one sheep, with the angel spreading its wings in all its brilliant white glory facing it. Or as glorious as human beings could make something with chalk, Teacher Rachel said.

"We can't copy the glory of real angels sent from a place as radiant as Heaven, where Jesus is now. But we can draw enough to inspire the people who come to the program, for sure."

The air was cold, with a stiff wind raking branches against the board fence, causing the horses tied there to be a bit skittish. The schoolhouse was lit with battery lamps and candles, children standing against the wall dressed in their best Christmas colors of red and green. Some of the lower graders were so wired with a case of nerves, they jumped randomly off the porch and dashed around the schoolhouse until Teacher Rachel rang the bell and they had to stay in their seats. This was no way to act at a Christmas program.

Mothers came through the door loaded down with gifts and Tupperware containers of cookies, bowls of snack mix and seasoned pretzels, cheese balls and crackers. There were huge coffee butlers with a spigot on one side that opened and closed very easily, five-gallon Igloos of tea or water, paper cups and plates, Christmas napkins and a red tablecloth. Babies fussed and were given to fathers, while mothers bent to remove bonnets, coats, and scarves. There was a general fuss about the blackboard.

"Oh my," Annie heard Ben Lapp sie Nancy say to Katie Stoltzfus. "It gives me chills, it looks so real."

"She is something," Katie said in a loud whisper.

"Give the glory to *der Herr*," was the gentle answer.

Their shoulders touched briefly in perfect understanding. This was Christmas, with inspiration everywhere you looked. The indescribable gift of the Messiah, revealed first to old and faithful Zechariah, who was a priest in the temple of Jerusalem, told that he and his wife Elizabeth would have a son, the forerunner to the man called Jesus. They heard it in church, they read it in their Bible, they told their children the story of Mary and Joseph from picture Bible stories. Solemnly, the children listened, thinking how they would certainly have given Him their room, their bed, when there was no room in the inn. Yes, they would, but as adults, they would often fail to give room in their hearts, which is the destiny of human beings, the battle of every Christian. But these two women touched shoulders and knew the gift of the Messiah in their hearts.

Finally, the room was full, the headlights off, the horses tired and blanketed in the wind. A few vehicles were parked along the opposite side of the playground, drivers accompanying their passengers into the classroom to see the program.

Fannie whispered to Annie that she might throw up. Annie told her to think pleasant thoughts, like of the Baby Jesus or bread with jelly on it. Fannie said she would try.

The small hand bell was tapped and the children filed quietly behind the curtain. Teacher Rachel took a deep breath, stood in the middle of the stage, and spoke in a clear, modulated voice.

"Thank you for coming to our program. The children have been practicing, working hard for your enjoyment, and we hope you will enjoy their efforts."

That was all, but it was enough. Annie wished she could have seen her, so slim and pretty, standing there all by herself in her red dress.

The whole class surged out of the curtain on both sides, singing "Joy to the World" with their whole hearts. It was a burst of joyous sound from a small group, but it was awesome, inspiring even the most jaded soul. A few discreet tears were wiped. Nancy and Katie touched shoulders and stayed there briefly, till Katie bent to get a baby wipe from her diaper bag.

My, those children could sing. And that blackboard. It was too much. Then Ruth read the second chapter of Luke, about the birth of the Baby Jesus. As an interesting touch, Teacher Rachel had Ruth read it in German, which took more practice, but was unique in its own way. Ruth was very smart, so German was easy, and her words were pronounced correctly, spoken clearly and precisely. Annie and Fannie smiled at each other, feeling proud of their sister. Ruth could be a genuine dear, even more so than Naomi, who secretly thought she was better than Ruth, which she wasn't.

Now it was Annie's turn to say her poem. She walked out, felt the duct tape marking her spot beneath her feet, and lifted her face to the back of the room, remembering to keep her words apart from one another and to speak loudly. Her poem had twelve verses about the wonders of Christmas, and were not hard to say. She'd said it so many times, the words tumbled out with no thought attached, so she walked behind the curtain with full confidence in her own ability to have done it right. Poems were easy. It was the plays that could mess you up.

The audience laughed at Fannie playing the part of Aunt Hattie, come to visit Aunt Petunia, all the children spying on them, then spreading their dubious gossip among the neighbors.

Oh, they were good.

The parents sat up, took notice. Here was a Christmas program unlike any they'd ever seen. Someone—and they knew it was Teacher Rachel— had worked extraordinarily hard. Pupils didn't come by this naturally.

There was a serious play, one about poverty and the Gift given to all mankind, a play done so well most mothers clutched their little ones and wiped one stray tear, then gave up and wept softly, honked into their Kleenexes and handkerchiefs and thought they'd go home and open their hearts and their checkbooks to every charity's solicitation they received in the mail. Ida Fisher felt a twinge in her innermost conscience when Amos Lantze's little boy forgave the miserly store manager in a particularly poignant skit. Was that how it really was? She'd have to go home and see what her tattered old Bible said about forgiveness, but she might have to think differently about her mother-in-law if she wanted to have Jesus in her heart the way these children portrayed it.

This program was something, now wasn't it? Wasn't it, though? And when they belted out the song "Go Tell It on the Mountain," parents tapped their feet and almost caught themselves nodding their heads, but realized quickly it wouldn't be acceptable.

Dat smiled and blew his nose, told his neighbor Daniel he'd never seen anything like this. Daniel nodded, said he believed they'd been blessed with Teacher Rachel.

But Naomi carried the whole program by her portrayal of Mammy, the mother with her disobedient son Rufus. Naomi was as smart as Ruth, with a lot of swagger and no inhibitions at all. She was good in programs, and she knew it, so she gave everything. The audience tittered, small giggles erupting like bubbles, till the part where he, Rufus, took off, scared of his own misdeeds, and Mammy lost it, stalking across the stage, swinging her arms and making all kinds of remarks. The men guffawed, the women laughed outright, and the play halted till the noise shut down, just the way they'd been taught.

The German version of "Silent Night" was sung slowly and softly by the upper grades, so touching they could almost feel the soft breeze and see the bright star in the velvety, pulsing night, alive with the birth of the Christ Child. "*Schtille Nacht, Helige Nacht.*"

Yes, it was a real treat, this wonderful Christmas program, and the audience was reluctant to accept the goodbye song. But there was coffee and hot chocolate, plates to be filled with Christmas treats, and visiting to do before they headed home in the cold darkness.

A refinished antique trunk decked out in ribbons and bows was carried in by the eighth grade boys, all of them bright-eyed and secretly infatuated with the lovely teacher. She put both hands to her mouth, her eyes open wide, and gave a little shriek.

"Oh my goodness! How did you know?" she gasped, and the boys were blessed beyond words. They had done something of great importance, pleased the teacher immensely, so all was right with their world.

She opened the lid and and small children crowded around to take a look. Printed fabric lined the interior, just the way the travelers of past centuries would have found it. She was truly pleased, so the children hopped up and down with sheer excitement. She thanked them all, her cheeks flushed and pretty, then read the card signed by all the parents. She received praise with humility, gave the honor to the children's abilities, then filled a cup with coffee and sat with the women.

Out on the porch, in the light from the window, Annie was discussing Christmas gifts with a group her age. They all wanted a football or an expensive aluminum baseball bat, the girls wanting calligraphy sets or Barbie dolls. Annie announced her wish for a riding horse, but Elam promptly dampened her spirits by saying she'd never get one. The price of a good horse was out of control.

Annie lifted her chin and asked what he knew about it.

"My dat went to a horse sale in Ohio, and the best horse fetched over a hundred thousand. Your dat doesn't have that kind of money."

"You don't say *fetched*. The Dutch word is *kolt*, which is *brought*," she fired back.

"Whatever," he said with a shrug.

"And another thing. You have no idea how much money my dat has. So what you don't know, don't say."

She took a deep breath and went back into the noisy, crowded classroom, filled another plate with cheese and squares of bologna, a cupcake, and some cheese curls, and went to sit with Mam, who turned to smile at her.

"Are you glad the program's over?" she asked kindly.

Annie nodded, ate her cupcake slowly, and felt as if someone had stuck a needle in her balloon of happiness. What did Elam know, really? He stretched stuff. He stretched it so far, it was an outright lie. He should be ashamed of himself. But the whole truth was she knew he was right. It seemed as if she kept building up her hope, and so quickly it was taken away. Maybe it would have been better to never want a horse, never mention it to Dat, who might not have any money for one.

She felt the Christmas spirit disappear. The cupcake turned dry in her mouth. She decided to see if Dat would eat the rest of her food, so she made her way over to where the men were seated along the wall. He was talking to a neighbor, Jesse King.

"So, they're doing alright?"

"Oh yeah. They'll be good to go till Christmas."

"You'll let me know what I owe you, then?"

"Sure will."

"Dat, do you want this?" Annie asked, handing the plate to him.

"Sure, you don't want it?"

Annie shook her head and walked away. She heard Jesse say something about telling those two apart, but she was used to it, so she didn't pay him any attention.

On the way home, Dat had his hands full driving the cold, impatient horse. Standing in the night air, horses all around stomping restlessly, chewing on boards, rattling the bits in their mouths had been hard, so now he wanted to run at top speed, which made Mam clench her teeth and her hands.

Naomi counted and recounted her successes, took all the applause for herself, talking on and on about how well everything went, which Dat and Mam endorsed by smiling and staying quiet. Ruth stepped up to the plate and said everyone did well, not just her, and Naomi got all huffy and said she knew that, she wasn't talking about just herself.

But she was. Annie knew she was. Fannie did, too.

But when Naomi's skirt caught on the brake pedal, and she was jerked off her feet, falling flat on her stomach on the cold, hard ground, and she yowled out her pain and embarrassment, Annie took pity on her. That was an awful blow to a person's pride, falling out of a buggy. You always had to watch out for that brake pedal and your skirt.

* * *

Back in school the following day, they helped Teacher Rachel take down the curtains and erase the blackboard and wash it clean with warm water and a microfiber cloth. The clean blackboard was kind of depressing until Teacher Rachel wrote the schedule for December 27, and she thought of coming back to school and being hard at work doing arithmetic, with no pressure of the Christmas program. And besides, you could have Christmas every day in your heart. Every single day. That was the nicest thought of all.

They swept the floor and got down on their hands and knees with buckets of hot, soapy water and clean cloths. Teacher Rachel dusted, burned trash, and worked alongside everyone, encouraging them by telling them they were certainly good helpers and how nice that trunk looked in her room.

So Annie felt better and thought how much nicer it was to give than to receive. She walked home beside Fannie and felt even better after all that cold, fresh air.

One more day before Christmas. Only one. Mam was like a whirlwind, cleaning, washing, baking, saying Mommy and Daudy Fisher and Aunt Elsie and Uncle Isaac were coming too, which that made twenty-one for dinner. Twenty-one people at the table, which was perfect. All the leaves in the table would stretch it out far enough to accommodate that many, with one to spare.

"Why twenty-one. It's only eighteen, Mam," Fannie said, always the practical one.

"Emanuel. Miriam. Sadie," Mam said, counting on her fingers slowly and thoroughly, as if those three were special ornaments on the tree in her life. Which they were.

Annie told Fannie when they were gathering eggs in the henhouse that three more added to the pile of brothers and sisters they already had, which only put them farther down on Mam's pole.

"It's not really fair being youngest. After all of them start dating we'll be buried under the whole pile. She won't even know we exist."

Fannie finished putting two eggs in the basket. She set the basket down slowly, then straightened and stood very close to Annie.

"Well, Annie, I know what you mean. But as long as we live, you'll be my twin, and I'll be yours. Which means when the going gets rough, we'll always have each other. Always."

"You're right, Fannie."

Fannie silently held up a hand, palm out. Annie smacked it lightly with her own. The sound frightened a brown hen, who ran squawking to the opposite corner, taking half of the chickens with her. Annie made an impatient sound, jerking a thumb in the direction of the chickens, rolling her eyes, but Fannie shook her head.

"Turkey poults are dumber," she said.

Annie nodded, then headed back to the house with the warm, brown eggs.

Mam was making raspberry jam strips when they got back to the house, muttering to herself as she rolled the dough into a long, thick rope. Her cheeks were flushed, her hair loose and sticking out in all directions, her covering crooked on her head. She was clearly in a dither, the way she kept tugging on her left ear.

"I thought you already made them," Annie said quietly, knowing Mam's dithers were something to be reckoned with.

"I did. But I don't have enough left. The boys get into the containers in the freezer, thaw them out, and munch away. But I guess they have to eat something."

"I guess."

"And this year, it's a bit nerve-wracking, thinking of having the three who are dating. It's something new. Something different, so I want everything perfect, which creates tension. Just my pride, I know."

She kept on talking, but Annie was only half listening. Why didn't she try to impress her own children? That was odd, getting all worked up about a boyfriend and two girlfriends. Emanuel wasn't anything to look at, though he was pretty special in other ways. And those girls. *Well, la-de-da*, Annie thought. She sure hoped Mike's Christmas every day would turn out alright. Sadie, Amos's girlfriend, seemed a safer bet. She was quiet and good natured, always spoke to her and Fannie, which meant she thought of others, not just herself.

Dating was funny business, really. You just went out on a limb and looked for someone you thought you wanted to spend the rest of your life with, then proceeded to spend time with them, getting to know them, before actually going ahead and having a wedding. All this time, you imagined your life to be perfect. Well, above average. Like Mike's Christmas every day.

She, Annie, would never do that. She would be a very pleasant single girl, living in a green house with white gingerbread trim. She would own two horses, one to drive and one to ride, named Sparkle and Fire. Or Spark and Fire. Maybe Sparkle and Fiery. Something like that. No henhouse. No chickens with anger issues. A dog named Bentley, but she'd pronounce it with the L all fancy, the way English people said it. She'd be a teacher like Rachel and decorate blackboards and have great Christmas programs and get paid an awful lot of money from the school board.

And she would never have twelve children with girlfriends and boyfriends coming home for Christmas dinner and have to make those troublesome jam strips to impress them. And she would certainly not marry a man who did nothing but smile and never made enough money to buy his twin daughters a horse.

They had poached eggs in milk with toast for supper, which was about as low as you could go. She hated poached eggs and refused to eat them. Mam said she guessed she'd have to eat cold cereal then.

"Whatever happened to good old Christmas spirit?" Amos asked.

"Oh, it's here. The gift of Christmas is everywhere," Mike answered.

They looked at each other, nodded and high-fived, then laughed out loud, all their teeth showing like rows of white corn.

Dat smiled, said it was beginning to look as if there would be a white Christmas this year. The paper said snow.

Everyone squealed, yelled, or clapped. Hands reached to the ceiling.

And that night, when the windows went dark and Mam and Dat knelt by their bed to pray, a few snowflakes slid onto the shingled roof and lay there till they melted into tiny drops of moisture. Thick clouds obscured the moon and all the stars as a few more flakes drifted down. In an hour or so, the frozen ground was covered in a thin layer of white, as if a giant, gauzy scarf had blown across the sky and settled across the countryside.

Pine trees held out their branches to relieve the sanctifying layer of pure white crystals, and squirrels curled up deep in the recesses of their nests. When the morning light awakened them, they'd look out with bright, unblinking eyes on the farmhouse below, watching as dark figures zigzagged from house to barn to calf hutches and the small henhouse.

They chattered among themselves as the familiar dark form emerged with a plastic bucket of sunflower seeds and one of peanuts to replenish the winter supply for her beloved birds and the squirrels she took pity on.

Chapter Eleven

AND IT WAS CHRISTMAS DAY. CHORES WERE done in record time, a breakfast of scrambled eggs and toast eaten as soon as possible. Dat was ushered to his chair, his Bible handed to him, and twelve children gathered round. There would be no presents without hearing the story of Christ's birth first and, he hoped, foremost.

The snow was an added blessing, an undeserved bonus, he said.

"Beautiful. Just beautiful," Mam said.

"Snowboarding!" the boys said.

Sarah worried about Emanuel's arrival later that day.

Dat's voice rose and fell, but probably the only one listening well was Mam, who wiped an occasional tear with the corner of her apron. Annie and Fannie kept turning their faces to the window, watching the snow, trying not to think of a horse.

To listen to this story, again, was just a little over-done in their opinion. They'd heard it every day for a month, knew the whole thing by heart, which meant it was losing its flavor. But it was traditional, and both Mam and Dat were real sticklers for that, so they listened.

Packages were handed out, starting with the twins, who were youngest, and it wasn't fair to make them wait till last. The big package was a Kan Jam game, and they were duly pleased. Another, smaller package contained two pairs of furry snow boots, with warm and silky insides, something they both needed badly.

Then on to Naomi and Ruth, who quietly opened their packages, being careful of the wrapping paper, too cool to crumple or rip it and yell with apprecia-tion the way they used to. They received new sweat-ers and fabric for new Sunday dresses, plus a plaque for their room with eucalyptus on it and a saying about home and family. They each got new boots too, like Annie and Fannie's, only nicer. That was really exciting, and for a moment, they forgot them-selves and shrieked a little bit.

More gifts, more siblings, each one happy to receive their special package, and then another. Rollerblades, skateboards, hunting knives, and pretty decor for the girls. A new duffel for Salome and shoes she seemed awfully pleased about. The list just went on and on.

After the gifts were all thoroughly examined, tried out, or put in upstairs rooms for safekeeping, Mam opened the oven door repeatedly to check on the Christmas ham, ensuring the flavor with added broth, adjusting the temperature.

Annie and Fannie put the Kan Jam game in the laundry room closet, then put on their new boots, just to try them out. *Oh my*, they both thought. *The nicest pair of boots ever.*

So in spite of feeling a bit disappointed about Christmas in general—thinking about a horse even if they tried no to—it was a good Christmas Day. All the family together, exchanging gifts, everyone in a good state of mind, was something. To feel loved and cherished by parents and siblings was worth a great deal.

Mike and Amos went upstairs to change into Sunday finery—red shirts, vests, and black trousers—then combed their hair in front of the downstairs laundry room mirror as if the exact placement of each strand of hair would secure their girlfriends' devotion. Annie and Fannie hung around the doorframe, trying not to give away their position, till Mike caught them and smiled.

"Do I look nice enough?"

"Not anything special," they teased.

Mam was peeling potatoes, her face pink with exertion. Becky was mixing corn with melted butter and crushed saltines, while Mary fried bacon for the salad. Mike and Amos were told to put the leaves in the table, which was always their chore. The table could be extended to accommodate twenty-four people, but there were only twenty-one that day, so a few boards could stay in the closet. A long white tablecloth was stretched on top, then a stack of plates were brought from the "combine." A hutch, actually, but Amish people called their hutches "combines." The dinner plates had a pattern of blue roses, and Annie thought them inappropriate for Christmas and asked Mam why they couldn't have Christmas plates if Mike and Amos's girlfriends were so fancy. Mam's face got that pinched conservative look she always wore when she disapproved of change, and she spoke in clipped tones when she told them her mother would never have bought Christmas plates, and she wasn't going to throw away good money on paper plates either.

Boy.

Annie and Fannie rolled their eyes behind her back, thought blue roses just didn't really make sense. But she did put three jar candles in the middle. Red ones, which looked very festive when they were lit. They put three sticks of butter on butter plates, homemade raspberry jelly in glass jelly dishes, all shiny and quivery and delicious on warm homemade dinner rolls.

Mam grew her own raspberries, the stalks as dangerous as any porcupine, with thorns up and down the bushes. Picking raspberries was a miserable job, reaching through thorns to get to the plump purple berries, your arms a mess of scratches crisscrossed like roads on a map, the sun hot on your back, and bees drunk with fermented berry juice flying like unguided missiles. Plus, it took a long time to fill the bottom of a small plastic ice cream bucket, filling it to the top a thought you couldn't entertain for long or depression would settle right in.

But on Christmas Day, Annie was grateful for the delicious jelly, plus there would be raspberry mush for dessert, that silky purple pudding you piled on top of chocolate cake with chocolate icing. It was so good and took away the sting of picking raspberries.

There would be a black walnut cake, too, with maple icing. Dat's favorite. In the fall, the girls picked up the green walnuts that fell from the old walnut tree beside the driveway. They poured the bucketfuls onto the cement slab by the laundry room door to let them dry, then removed the outer husk before cracking the hard brown shell with a nutcracker and removing the large, tender nut meats inside. Daudy and Mommy Fisher cracked almost all of them in their small house in winter, bringing glass gallon jars of shelled walnuts for Mam, who used them up in her baking.

But the date pudding was from store-bought dates, because they grew in a faraway land in clusters hanging down from date palms. Harvesters climbed ladders or used special lifts to reach the clusters high up in the trees, and they picked the fruit by hand. These dates were packaged and sent to the United States, Salome said, who read anything she could get her hands on, then told the rest of the family everything she read.

Date pudding was actually a cake made with sugar and butter and eggs, except it contained two cups of cut-up dates and a cup and a half of walnuts, chopped fine. The cake was cut in tiny pieces and layered with a rich caramel sauce and whipped cream in a glass dish Mam called a trifle dish. When Fannie asked why it was called a trifle dish, she said she guessed it was trifling, then giggled till her stomach shook up and down. Mam was always kind of silly when she made fancy desserts, which seemed to make her happy.

There would be fruit salad, too, with home-canned peaches and pears, plus fresh pineapple bits, sliced strawberries, oranges, kiwi slices, and grapes, all bought from Aldi, Mam's favorite store. The whole salad was drizzled with a lemon sauce sweetened with sugar.

And pies, of course. Pumpkin pie, pecan pie, and chocolate pie with shaved chocolate on top of the whipped cream. So many delicious pies that there would be plenty of leftovers, which would be stored in the basement refrigerator for days after Christmas. That was just fine with Mam, knowing they would never go to waste.

The boys' horses pranced up the driveway, bringing their girlfriends to the Christmas dinner. Mam began breathing faster, going to the mirror to smooth her hair and adjust her covering. When the laundry room door opened, there was a general rustling of outerwear being removed, quiet voices. Mam calmed herself with a deep breath, then went to greet the girls with a smile and a handshake.

"*Kommet rye. Machet eich daheem.*" ("Come right in. Make yourselves at home.")

The girls were just a sight, decked out in silver dresses. Actually, it was true. Their dresses were identical shiny light gray fabric. Oh my, they were pretty.

They shone, even making Mike and Amos look better. Then Emanuel appeared with Sarah, and they were both dressed in red, which was good for Sarah, but not Emanuel. He was just so red. His hair and his face and his shirt. The only things keeping him from looking like a Red Delicious apple were his black vest and trousers and his white teeth flashing when he smiled, which was almost always.

For a while, Mam's face had that pinched look, which meant she was struggling with those silver dresses and the fact the girls were here at all, a serious breach of tradition. She would never have been invited to her boyfriend's family for Christmas, and here she was, inviting those fancy girls into her home. Well, for better or for worse, this was how it was now, and she had to accept it. Times changed.

Emanuel offered to mash the potatoes.

Mam's mouth hung open a few seconds longer than necessary. A man offering to mash potatoes? What? She hardly knew how to respond, but smiled and said, "Why sure."

Sarah simpered and giggled and smiled, offered a turn, but he refused. Mam put butter, salt, and cream cheese in the kettle of steaming potatoes, then made the ham gravy and began dishing up the baked corn, the lima beans, and buttered noodles.

Dat sliced the ham while the girls poured cold water into glasses. Salome filled two baskets with warm rolls and everyone found their name tag on their plate.

Dat smiled widely, then his eyes turned serious.

"We want to thank God for our meal now, but let's remember the Christ child, the most indescribable gift of all. For this, we honor the day, His birthday."

Mam's eyes were instantly watery, the way they always got whenever the birth of Jesus was mentioned. Fannie said it was Mam's soft heart; she pitied the Baby Jesus being born in a cold stable with no clothes to put on Him. Annie said the stable might not be cold, as Bethlehem was far away in a warmer country, but Fannie said she had no idea if it was warm or cold. They asked Salome, who said it had to be warm, with the shepherds on the hillside with their sheep, but it was a desert country, so the nights were likely cool. Not winter cold, but cool.

Oh, what a Christmas dinner it was. No one thought of blue roses on the plates, but helped themselves to all the dishes as they were handed up and down the table. The ham was tender and smoked just right, the mashed potatoes buttery and tasty. Everything was delicious, except for the lima beans, which were disgusting little orbs that popped open to reveal grainy white insides that smelled like skunk cabbage, that velvety plant growing in wet spots by the creek.

Mike talked too much, Annie thought, but evidently Miriam was okay with it. She put her shoulder against his and acted as if he was the best thing that ever happened to her. Sadie was quieter, but kept exchanging meaningful glances with Amos, who was also not given to excessive conversation.

Emanuel, though, was the star of the show. He glowed. He cracked jokes, really funny ones, even for Mam. Dat laughed and leaned back in his chair, clearly delighted at his prospective son-in-law. And Sarah? Well, Sarah looked as if the Star of Bethlehem shone from inside her. She glowed. She smiled. She cast appreciative glances full of sincerity. So many

lonely Sunday nights for them both. Almost five
years he had cared for his mother, provided for her,
and Sarah had not dated anyone else, had thought of
him and only him. This was, indeed, a modern day
Old Testament story, and the whole family hoped to
remember this gift.

The dessert plates were brought, followed by the
wonderful layer cake, the date pudding and pies, the
raspberry mush and fruit salad. Mam received praise
graciously, soaked up Dat's warm words for her, then
washed dishes with them all, put away the leftovers,
and sat beside Dat to sing Christmas carols, her voice
rising strong and true above his deep bass.

They sang "Stille Nacht" and "Kommet Alle"
then a rousing rendition of "Freve Dich Velt," the
German "Joy to the World." They sang "What Child
Is This?"—a relatively new one, but sung low and
slow, quietly beautiful with the harmony of many
voices.

Now it was time to play games, but there was a
sense of hesitation, a charged atmosphere, as if they
were all waiting for someone's appearance. Becky and
Mary were missing, Annie noticed. Dat yawned, but

the yawn wasn't quite normal, as if he'd forced it and it hadn't turned out right. Mam fidgeted with the corner of her apron, then looked at Dat.

"Annie and Fannie, why don't you get the lemonade out on the back porch?" he asked. "The jug's pretty heavy."

They obeyed immediately, the way they'd been taught, and slid off their chairs and hurried to the porch. Fannie pushed open the door, with Annie on her heels. The cold air hit their faces as they bent to take up the jug of lemonade.

"Hey!"

They turned. Their eyes opened wide as comprehension soaked in. Becky, wearing her black coat and white scarf, was leading a horse, with Mary's colorful blue scarf showing up a few steps behind her, leading another one. Exactly the same horse, except there were two.

They were almost pushed off the porch by the whole family bursting through the door, cheering and clapping, a great chorus of voices propelling them down the steps and out the walkway to stand in disbelief, unable to reach out and take the lead ropes.

Becky was laughing, saying, "Come on. Come on, take the rope."

Mary had to reach out and yank at her sleeve.

"But why two? Whose are they?" Annie asked when she finally found her voice.

"Yours. They're yours," Mary yelled, then burst into tears.

They were round and compact, golden in color, with cream-colored manes and tails. The twins had never seen a real live Haflinger, but here they were, the ultimate Christmas gift they'd longed for.

They cried, they laughed. They shouted happily. They stroked the warm soft necks beneath the heavy manes, touched the velvety noses, stood back, and looked into their wide eyes with the long lashes. These little horses were too good to be true. They almost expected them to evaporate into thin air, like a mist or a dream.

But they took the lead ropes and led them away, shivering now from the cold and excitement. Amos brought their coats, laughing as he handed them over. Dat said they came from a rescue farm, a place that saved horses from the kill pen, and he had purchased them at a reasonable price, fed them minerals and good feed, hay and water, over in Jesse King's barn. They were ten or twelve years old, the vet said, after a thorough exam.

"They're rescued horses, meant just for you. Now you can learn to ride. We have saddles and bridles for you, too."

They opened the big sliding barn doors and there they were, the saddles looking worn, but clean and brown, the bridles beside them. Annie was speechless, but Fannie turned around and looked her parents in the eyes and said solemnly, "*Denke. Denke, Mam und Dat.*"

Everyone crowded around to help them with the saddles, the horses both calm and accepting of the bit, standing quietly till the girls climbed up, waiting while Dat adjusted the stirrups. At first, he led them around the driveway until the girls said they'd like to try it by themselves, then rode proudly as everyone clapped and cheered.

That Christmas Day was the most memorable one of their lives. They spent all afternoon in the barn, long after the rest of the family returned to the warmth of the living room.

And they talked. Oh, how they chattered and laughed.

They groomed their horses with the brushes the boys used on their driving horses. For a long time, they discussed the best names for them. Dat said they had papers, meaning they already had registered names, but that he was sure the horses wouldn't mind if the girls wanted to choose their own.

"Goldie," Fannie said.

Annie shook her head, saying every single animal, dog, car, or horse of this color was named Goldie.

"What about Gingerbread?"

Annie stepped back to admire the combed mane, then began untangling the long forelock. She stroked the white blaze down the horse's face and said, "I love you, Horse. I just love you."

Fannie snorted, said she couldn't call him Horse.

"I know what. They're Haflingers. So something starting with H."

"No, that's too hard. Harry? You want a horse named Harry?"

"I didn't say Harry."

And so they continued into the late afternoon, when the sun slanted through the dusty barn windows and turned the horses' coats to gold. They were still brushing, mounting and dismounting, practicing throwing the saddle blanket on the patient horses' backs, followed by the saddle, even coaxing the bit into their opened mouths.

Suddenly, there was no sun. The forebay turned a gloomy gray. Annie ran to the milkhouse for a battery lamp and Fannie said they had to decide on names, it was getting late, and wasn't it supposed to snow more?

So they put both horses in the clean box stall provided for them, gave them a measure of oats and a block of hay, checked to make sure the automatic water trough Dat had installed for his livestock that summer worked properly. They put away their curry combs and brushes, hung the saddles and bridles on the board Dat had built for them, then stood back and shook their heads in wonder.

"Did this really happen? Is it true?"

"It is very true. We have the best family anyone ever had. We are two lucky girls. We have each other, and now we each have a horse."

"Tonight, when I say my prayers, I'm going to be very serious about being a better girl. I'm never going to get mad at Ruth and Naomi. Not ever again."

Annie nodded in total agreement. The two of them stood solemnly side by side in the darkening barn, the light from the battery lamp creating long shadows on the wall as they contemplated this state of gratitude. This was serious business, being horse owners, and if they were good girls, they could enjoy them for a very long time.

"I know what. We'll call them Happiness and Joy," Fannie said, quite unexpectedly.

"Joy would work, but Happiness is too long for a horse."

"What about Love?"

"That's just so mushy. Kind of overboard, if you know what I mean."

They took up the lantern and walked along the aisle to open the door to the stall and visit the two perfect horses one more time before going inside.

The horses both walked over and nudged them with their soft noses, and the girls put their arms around their necks, hugging them tightly.

"Their manes and tails are the color of taffy. You know. When we pull that stuff Mam cooks and it starts out a dark brown, and suddenly it's light tan in color."

"Oh yeah. Sure. We'll call them Taffy."

"They can't both be called that."

"I know. Honey!"

"Honey and Taffy!"

"But they're boys. They're geldings. We can't name them after candy."

They decided, with the ever-decreasing light, they'd return to the house and think about horses' names, perhaps enlist the help of the family. When they opened the door and the wind tugged at their skirts, bits of snow pelted their faces. Annie said, "Stormy," and Fannie said, "Windy," and those were the names given to the Christmas horses.

Chapter Twelve

INSIDE, THE HOUSE WAS WARM, ALIVE WITH the sounds of Christmas everywhere. Board games, caramel popcorn, a fresh pot of coffee on the stove, Mam washing mugs and making hot chocolate, smiling and humming as she fairly burst with goodwill.

Here was her family, all together as one, with a bright cloud of upcoming proposals, married children and grandchildren just on the horizon. Generations after her would benefit from the efforts, the hard work of maintaining the ties that bind, the beloved traditions she held so dear. Yes, yes, Miriam and Sadie might be a little fancy for her taste, but she had done her best to instill old values in her children, to teach them to live lives of honesty and integrity, to go to church and respect their elders. It was all so precious, these dear children. How could a mother ever convey the depth and the height of her love?

And here came Annie and Fannie, bursting through the laundry room door reeking to high heaven from those horses, their good black coats gray with dust and covered in horse hair. Her twins. Their twins. The discomfort of carrying them, the pain of childbirth, the utter exhaustion of sleepless nights for her and Ben, and here they were, the delight of their lives. A true blessing.

So she didn't scold, as she might have done another time, but smiled as they entered the kitchen and asked them to wash their hands before they snacked on Christmas treats.

They all noticed the wind picking up, rattling the loose bit of gutter on the north corner of the house. Dat got up from the Woods and Water game, poked more wood into the stove, and opened the draft a bit. Miriam donned her sweater, saying she was chilly, and Mike asked if she wanted to leave. Emanuel opened the front door to take a look outside and was taken aback by the force of the wind, the pelting snow flying into the room with surprising velocity.

"Wow! Looks like it's time for me to hit the road, or not hit it at all. This is a serious storm," he said, turning to Sarah.

Annie and Fannie nodded to each other. Windy and Stormy.

So the wonderful Christmas Day came to an abrupt end, with three buggies wending their way out the drive, lights blinking in the back, headlights slicing through the whirling white snow, the dark horses trotting steadily.

Mam stewed and worried, but Dat assured her the horses were all traffic safe if they did meet a snow-plow, and Emanuel seemed a safe bet with a horse. Sarah smiled quietly, nodded, and sang a song to herself as she began to wash dishes.

Annie and Fannie helped themselves to mugs of hot chocolate, piled a plate with Rice Krispie treats and party mix, a few chocolate cookies, and some fruit salad in a dish. They both talked at once, telling everyone the names of their horses, how well behaved they were, then turned to Dat and properly thanked him, then their mother, who nodded and smiled happily.

"Dat, you must tell us the story of how you bought them."

He propped the kitchen broom against the wall, came over, and sat with them, helping himself to a handful of party mix.

"Well, I'd heard about this place, but wasn't sure I believed everything going around, so Ron Mailer and I went to check it out. It's a fairly decent-looking place, about thirty miles from here, over toward Howard. You can tell it's run on donations, some of the buildings could use some repairs. But what it is, it's simply a series of barns and sheds housing horses slated for the kill pen or mistreated ones someone reported to authorities. Your two horses were together in one pen, and I must say I have never seen a sadder set of animals. Their necks were thin, their ribs showing, just a terribly scraggly coat, all over poor health. I had their teeth floated, wormed them, and fed them real good. Jesse's boys worked them since October sometime. They still have a way to go, though." He grinned. "So you like them, do you?"

They laughed, said, "What do you think?"

Ruth and Naomi crowded around, listening to Dat's story and, for once, were not jealous of all the attention. They were not horse lovers, had no interest in the equine world, so they could simply be happy for their younger siblings. "For once," Annie told Fannie later, but was duly warned, reminding her they were going to be the best they'd ever been, after that surprise.

* * *

Evening chores were done in the blinding snow, scarves wrapped around their heads and over their faces. The barn itself was warm enough, the heat from the animals providing some comfort, the sturdy walls keeping out the wind-driven snow, but Annie and Fannie had calves to feed and eggs to gather. About halfway through feeding calves, Annie had a bright idea, slipped and slid through the snow, and returned with an umbrella, a huge black affair they took along on the spring wagon in case of a summer thunderstorm.

That was a great plan, it really was, the way the large black expanse protected them from the worst of it. They rinsed out the buckets, hung them upside down on the rack, and scurried quickly, struggling to open the henhouse door, the battery lamp creating a whirling white expanse of snowflakes zooming in from the north.

The chickens were easily spooked, cold, and grouchy. A big brown hen pecked Fannie's hand hard, hard enough to make her squeal in protest.

"You get her, Annie."

"Should have kept your gloves on," Annie commented dryly, reaching under the puffed-up, baleful-eyed chicken, finding one leg and drawing her out to fling her into a corner.

"You're not nice to chickens," Fannie observed.

"They're not nice to us. They peck our hands for no reason."

"Duh. We're taking their eggs."

Through the blinding snow, two sets of headlights slowly came up the road and turned in at the end of the driveway. The girls watched from the henhouse door, then breathed a collective sigh. It was good to know their brothers had made a safe return, the way this snowstorm was increasing its power.

They went to bed on Christmas Day with the happy thought of being brand-new, genuine horse owners, an overwhelming amount of love for their family, and the sense of being blessed beyond measure. They rode their horses in their dreams and awoke on second Christmas to find the snow still whirling through the gray clouds, creating a white light that seemed to hurt your eyes even if the sun wasn't shining.

Second Christmas was *Tzvet Grischtag* in Pennsylvania Dutch. It was, essentially, an extension of Christmas Day to allow for more Christmas dinners with extended family. Another day of visiting, eating, and drinking, continuing to spread the Christmas cheer.

They had a family dinner on Dat's side of the family and a Christmas singing in the evening, so Mam had been up early, mopping floors, doing laundry, gathering leftovers into containers, and mixing a big batch of stuffing to take along.

The snow had piled up during the night, so the girls' new boots were put to good use as they followed the shoveled path to the barn. Both horses nickered softly at sight of them, and they smiled, clearly delighted to be recognized after such a short time.

"Another Christmas!" Dat sang out.

"It's Christmas every day with our horses," they sang back.

And Dat's smile turned into a loud laugh.

The twins were clearly the apple of his eye, the feather in his cap of life, the crowning jewel of the large number of children around his table, a blessing for his wife and him as they aged.

Surely God had been good and would continue to be faithful until the end of their lives.

* * *

The girls rode the horses almost every day.

In spring, their hooves pounded through the mud. In summer, they spit dry gravel onto dusty weeds by the side of the road. In the autumn, they rode beneath gorgeous displays of changing leaves, their horses' hooves puffing up carpets of fallen gold, orange, and brown. They raced uphill and down on freshly mowed hayfields and fallow fields of brown weeds ripe with unpicked wild strawberries. They hitched them double to a wheeled cart and learned to trick ride, until Mam said no more.

To be seated on a horse, with or without a saddle, was an incredible feeling. At first, it seemed as if the ground below was alarming in its distance, but that fear evaporated in time. The steady drumming of hooves, the strength in the muscular bodies beneath them, the flowing manes in their faces was indescribable, the best thing in all the world.

Emanuel proposed that spring, on Easter holiday, and Sarah said, "Yes, oh yes, we've waited so long!" Or at least that's what Mam told Ruth and Naomi, who were all goggle-eyed at the thought of their sister getting married. So Sarah walked around with an eternally pleased expression, and Emanuel simply turned pinker in summer.

Mam was floating around in the clouds somewhere, planning a wedding—a real, live wedding for one of her girls. Would wonders never cease?

She and Sarah sat around with a spiral notebook and muttered about cousins and aunts and uncles and ministers and church districts, engrossed in their own little world of wedding planning.

By now, Mam was developing a nervous tic in her left eye and had to take calm tablets, which had a large dose of magnesium in them, and she had to run to the restroom a lot. So Annie and Fannie realized they were pretty much on their own, the way things were shaping up with the older ones, and began riding bareback, playing Indians and pioneers, standing on their horses' backs while they galloped, holding on to a single rope.

Till Mam found out, anyway.

That next September, after they'd owned the horses almost two years and were in sixth grade, things really got out of control, with Sarah's wedding on the second of November, Mike and Miriam on the twenty-third, and Amos and Sadie sometime in December—they couldn't be sure on account of her sister expecting her first baby. Luckily, Mam didn't have to do three weddings, only one, Sarah being a daughter. The twins agreed, Mam likely couldn't get through three weddings in one year, so she was lucky Amos and Mike had been boys.

Allen Kauffman dated Becky's best friend, Barbie Ann, then broke up with her about six months later, waited a decent length of time, and then asked Becky to go to his carpenters' Christmas diner. She told him yes, sewed a terribly fancy gold dress, and went, Mam wringing her hands and lamenting the state of the world and fabric in general. Where had she gone wrong with Becky? Awful, just awful, the way she rolled her hair. She hemmed and hawed at Becky, but she might as well have been a Chihuahua puppy yapping away, for all the good it did.

But on Emanuel and Sarah's wedding day, Becky was *nāva sitza*, or "beside-sitter," which meant she was an attendant, part of the bridal party. Dressed in blue, with a white cape and apron, her hair sprayed, wetted, and rolled into subjection, she looked quite presentable, and Mam wept a bit in pure relief.

It was, indeed, a gorgeous fall day, the service tender and very spiritual, Mam sniffing demurely into her handkerchief and Dat trying to appear gruff and stern, failing miserably, giving up, and honking into his handkerchief as emotion overtook him. It was so touching, the story of Emanuel and Sarah, how he'd served his mother five years before asking Sarah, trusting in God all that time.

The entire day was a celebration of true love, God's blessing radiating everywhere. Annie and Fannie were too young to be with the youth, but it was immensely interesting, watching the day's proceedings.

Afterward, they went riding down the back field lanes and into the sun-dappled woods that lay between their farm and Joe Willis's, and Fannie told Annie she was getting married after all. Someday.

Annie glared back at her and asked why. Whatever for? She knew the rest of her life she'd be bowing to a husband and having a whole pile of babies, and what if her husband didn't have any money and she had to wash cloth diapers and cook oatmeal? Annie wasn't going to. She was fully planning on having a horse farm. She'd changed her mind about teaching school. It was all about horses for her.

They helped Sarah move her things into Emanuel's house, the house where he'd cared for his mother. The house she died in, which gave Annie a dark feeling, as if death were a shadow on the wall or something. But she didn't tell Sarah, not wanting to hurt her feelings. Besides, she'd painted the walls, so that was good.

Then, Mike and Miriam were married on the Tuesday before Thanksgiving, and the wedding went off without a hitch. Miriam looked plain and subdued, so that stroked Mam's pride, and she became very supportive and loving throughout the day. At least until she found out through Salome they'd rented an Airbnb in the mountains of Kentucky somewhere for a honeymoon, which was so out of the *ordnung* and so terribly uncalled for. Such a waste of money. Mike might as well have thrown hundreds of dollars in the river and watched it float away. Dat agreed but reminded her kindly that this was none of her business. The children were adults and made their own decisions now.

She had to say a few words to Mike, and he listened, then told his mother that some changes were good ones, and he was sure he would always cherish the memories of his honeymoon, and perhaps she should have had one, too.

She said, "Pooh," and flounced off in a huff.
Annie and Fannie saw it all and heard it, too. They
laughed about it, wondering how long Mam would
stay mad at Mike. Likely not very long.

Then, Amos and Sadie were married the seven-
teenth of December, a week and one day away from
Christmas. She had a Christmas wedding, decorated
with greens and candles, much too fancy for Mam,
but intriguing for Annie and Fannie. Amos looked
very handsome, they thought, and Sadie so sweet and
dear and quiet. It was a memorable day for everyone,
and very special, even if it was the third one in the
family.

At least they didn't rent an Airbnb, which gave
Mam hope that the rest of her children would not
follow in such a wasteful and worldly practice.

* * *

So now the family had shrunk to nine children, and
Becky was on the path to matrimony, evidently.
Mam took long naps on the recliner, refinished a few
dressers, went shopping for sheet sets and towels for

Mike and Amos and their wives, helped them move into their houses, dusted her hands of all that fancy *ga-mach* they had strewn all over their walls and tops of furniture. Times were changing and she would have to make peace with it.

Dat nodded, patted her shoulder, and she felt justified, for now. Annie and Fannie were in their last year of school when Becky got married and moved out of the house, which allowed them each a bedroom. They never slept alone, though, one or the other climbing into the other's bed.

They became legendary riders and eventually taught other young girls the tricks of being an extraordinary horseperson. After some years, when the chunky little Haflingers were getting too old to ride, they acquired two brown Morgans, half-trained rebels no one seemed to be able to gentle. They accomplished this in record time, rode the beautiful animals at the local horse auction, and were swarmed with offers. Confused, they were a bit out of their league with these grown English men offering them huge sums of money to train this horse or that one. So Dat helped them negotiate, taught them how to bargain with horse dealers, realized their lack of fear, their potential, and got them started on a lengthy career.

They stayed on the farm, trained one horse after another, and both agreed, it was like Christmas every day.

They loved horses, loved to work with them, grew strong and athletic, skilled in their field. The seasons came and went, more of their siblings were married and moved away, and they joined the group of youth when the proper time arrived. But they showed much more enthusiasm for their line of work than their weekend gatherings.

Dat and Mam's hair turned gray, their faces lined, and they enjoyed each grandchild as they arrived, everyone counting them a blessing as they had appreciated the birth of their own children. Mam often contemplated her large brood's lives and thought about changes presenting themselves and how miserable she actually was if she resisted them. Years ago, those twins would never have been allowed to train horses, to receive money from Amish and English alike, to be a part of a fast-growing industry.

Goodness, she pondered on the porch swing on a hot summer afternoon as she sat snapping green beans. *Goodness sakes. These girls will never marry. I don't believe they will.*

She heard the thundering hoofbeats, watched as Annie came flying up the drive on some snorting buckskin the size of a buffalo, winced as she drew back hard on the reins. She stopped the horse, turned to call out, "Mam, we're going to the game lands to ride!" before the horse reared, up and up, still farther, till Mam got up off the swing, a hand to her gasping mouth, green beans scattered everywhere, crying out, "Annie!"

And then she slid out of the saddle, across the horse's haunches, and sat down hard with a teeth-rattling thump. She leaped to her feet and ran after the runaway horse, catching up with him when he stopped at the hitching rack.

Mam sat back down on the porch swing, shook her head and muttered to herself.

This modern life was okay, she supposed, but don't come crying to me if you get hurt. But still, wasn't she a little proud of the twins? Sam Zook sie

Katie told her the twins intimidated the boys, that no one would ask them to date given the way they trained horses, and Mam realized she'd been secretly glad. She sincerely hoped the girls would hang on to her faith, to know tradition till the end, but yes, she'd been secretly proud of her girls' strength and skills.

She smiled to herself and snapped a green bean harder than necessary.

* * *

Annie and Fannie rode their charging, half-broke mounts into the golden evening when the sweet smell of summer roses hung thick in the air. A breeze brought the gentle rustling of oak leaves, the shadows played hide and seek with the sun, and they were content, for now. Perhaps not always, but just for today, joy and anticipation was like Christmas when they were children.

They would never forget the surprise Haflingers, and no one knew the spark that would ignite a true talent, a gift. But that was from God, the Giver of every good and perfect gift, so they couldn't heap piles of honor on their own heads.

But, my, they were something, those twins, everyone said. And so unassuming, so humble. Lucky were the young men who would ever win their hearts. Sometimes, when they rode, they winked at each other, or fist bumped, one knowing the other's thoughts. It didn't get any better than this.

Christmas came just once a year, it was true, but the spirit of love and gratitude, of giving from the heart, could be felt every single day you lived. You took the joy and the disappointment of life and rolled it all together into a nice package, wrapped it with courage, tied it with the ribbon of faith, attached a tag of love, and kept it beneath the Christmas tree of grace.

And as the horses' hooves pounded the red earth, they leaned forward and signaled for the race, the breathtaking race called life.

THE END

About the Author

LINDA BYLER WAS RAISED IN AN AMISH FAMILY and is an active member of the Amish church today. Growing up, Linda loved to read and write. In fact, she still does. Linda is well known within the Amish community as a columnist for a weekly Amish newspaper. She writes all her novels by hand in notebooks.

Linda is the author of several series of novels, all set among the Amish communities of North America: Lizzie Searches for Love, Sadie's Montana, Lancaster Burning, Hester's Hunt for Home, the Dakota Series, The Long Road Home, New Directions, and the Buggy Spoke Series for younger readers. Linda has also written several Christmas romances set among the Amish: *Mary's Christmas Goodbye*, *The Christmas Visitor*, *The Little Amish Matchmaker*, *Becky Meets Her Match*, *A Dog for Christmas*, *A Horse for Elsie*, *The More the Merrier*, *A Christmas Engagement*, and *Love Conquers All*. Linda has coauthored *Lizzie's Amish Cookbook: Favorite Recipes from Three Generations of Amish Cooks!*, *Amish Christmas Cookbook*, and *Amish Soups & Casseroles*.

OTHER BOOKS BY
LINDA BYLER

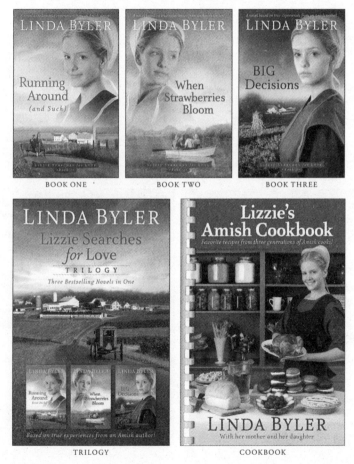

SADIE'S MONTANA SERIES

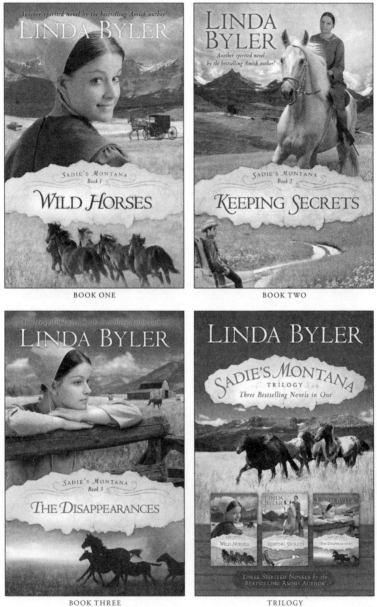

BOOK ONE

BOOK TWO

BOOK THREE

TRILOGY

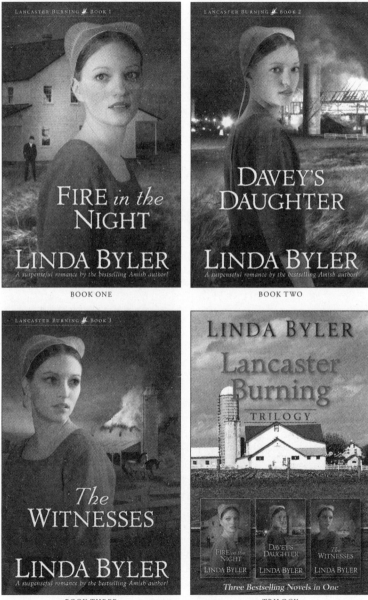

BOOK ONE

BOOK TWO

BOOK THREE

TRILOGY

HESTER'S HUNT FOR HOME SERIES

BOOK ONE

BOOK TWO

BOOK THREE

TRILOGY

BOOK ONE

BOOK TWO

BOOK THREE

TRILOGY

Long Road Home Series

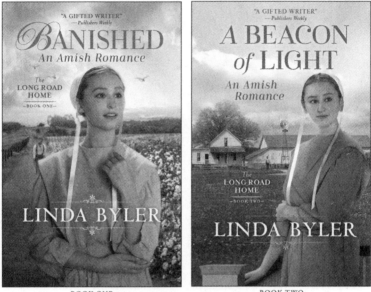

BOOK ONE

BOOK TWO

BOOK THREE

NEW DIRECTIONS SERIES

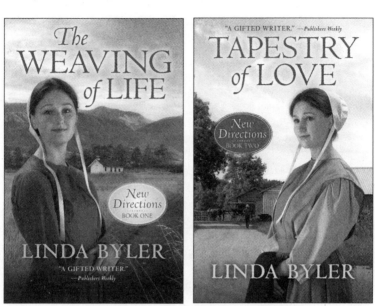

BOOK ONE

BOOK TWO

COMING SOON

BOOK THREE

Christmas Novellas

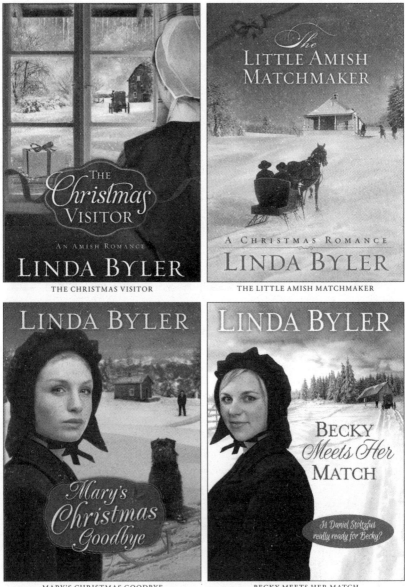

THE CHRISTMAS VISITOR

THE LITTLE AMISH MATCHMAKER

MARY'S CHRISTMAS GOODBYE

BECKY MEETS HER MATCH

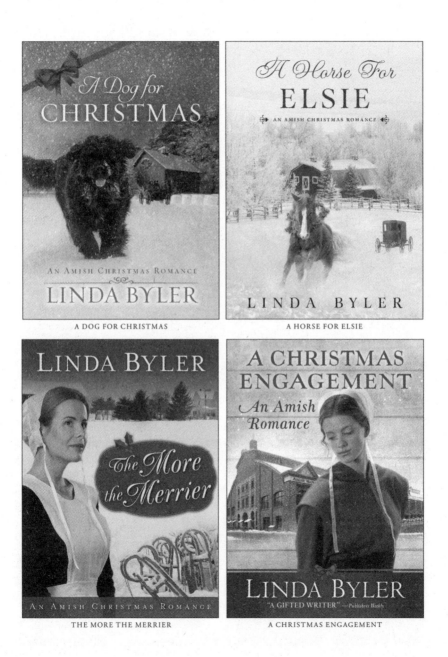

A DOG FOR CHRISTMAS

A HORSE FOR ELSIE

THE MORE THE MERRIER

A CHRISTMAS ENGAGEMENT

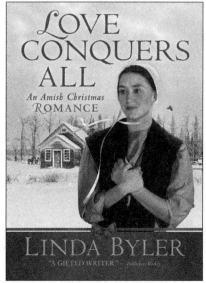

LOVE CONQUERS ALL

CHRISTMAS COLLECTIONS

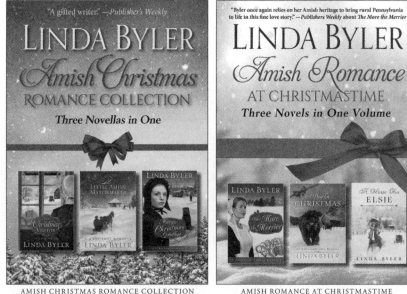

AMISH CHRISTMAS ROMANCE COLLECTION   AMISH ROMANCE AT CHRISTMASTIME

STANDALONE NOVELS

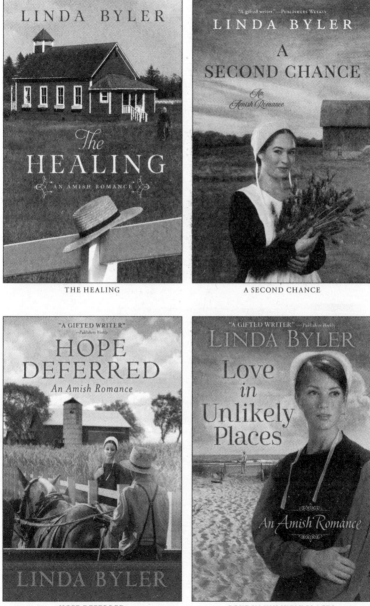

THE HEALING

A SECOND CHANCE

HOPE DEFERRED

LOVE IN UNLIKELY PLACES

BUGGY SPOKE SERIES FOR YOUNG READERS

BOOK ONE

BOOK TWO

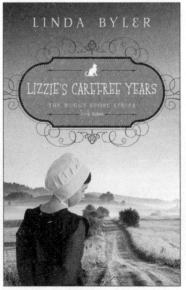

BOOK THREE